John Bodenham, und Andere

England's Helicon

A Collection of Lyrical and Pastoral Poems

John Bodenham, und Andere

England's Helicon
A Collection of Lyrical and Pastoral Poems

ISBN/EAN: 9783744763448

Printed in Europe, USA, Canada, Australia, Japan

Cover: Foto ©Andreas Hilbeck / pixelio.de

More available books at **www.hansebooks.com**

ENGLAND'S HELICON.

NOTE.—*Five hundred copies of this book printed, each of which is numbered as issued.*

No. 23.

ENGLAND'S HELICON.

A COLLECTION OF

LYRICAL AND PASTORAL POEMS:

PUBLISHED IN 1600.

EDITED BY

A. H. BULLEN.

LONDON:

JOHN C. NIMMO,

14, KING WILLIAM STREET, STRAND, W.C.

1887.

CHISWICK PRESS:—C. WHITTINGHAM AND CO., TOOKS COURT,
CHANCERY LANE.

PREFACE.

TWO or three years ago my friend Mr. W. J. Craig, an enthusiastic lover of Elizabethan poetry, announced his intention of editing *England's Helicon;* but, finding that his engagements did not allow him to redeem his promise, he requested me to undertake the work and generously placed his notes at my disposal. It had been Mr. Craig's intention to edit the anthology elaborately; but I have thought it best to make my introductory notice as brief as possible.

I take this opportunity of saying that I am preparing a *Second Series* of *Lyrics from Elizabethan Song-books.* I am particularly anxious to see Robert Jones' song-book, *The Muses' Garden for Delights,* 1611, from which Beloe gives extracts in the sixth volume (1812) of his *Anecdotes;* and I should be very grateful to any reader who would help me to discover this lost treasure.

Ultimately I hope to examine all the MS. collections of Elizabethan poetry preserved in public libraries, and make a collection of choice unpublished lyrics. This has been a cherished scheme of mine for many years.

31st March, 1887.

INTRODUCTION.

THE first English anthology, known as *Tottel's Miscellany,*[1] was published in 1557 and reached an eighth edition in 1587. Surrey and Wyatt were represented most largely; and among the other contributors were Sir Francis Bryan, Lord Vaux, Nicholas Grimoald, John Heywood, and Tom Churchyard. Michael Drayton in his admirable epistle to Henry Reynolds alludes, in terms of genial appreciation, to

> "those small poems which published were
> Of *Songs and Sonnets,* wherein oft they hit
> On many dainty passages of wit."

Master Slender,[2] it will be remembered, was a diligent reader of the old anthology.

In 1576 appeared *The Paradise of Dainty*

---

[1] *Songes and Sonettes, written by the ryght honorable Lorde Henry Haward late Earle of Surrey, and other. Apud Richardum Tottel,* 1557.

[2] "I had rather than forty shillings I had my book of *Songs and Sonnets* here."—*Merry Wives,* i. 1.

Devices, which passed through eight editions in twenty-four years. The editor (and largest contributor) was Richard Edwards, a scholar and courtier, author of an unreadable old play, *Damon and Pythias,* 1571. Among the contributors were Edward Vere Earl of Oxford, Lord Vaux, W. Hunnis, John Heywood, and Francis Kindlemarsh (or Kinwelmersh). There is good poetry in the collection, but the quality varies considerably.

The third anthology, *A Gorgeous Gallery of Gallant Inventions,* edited by a certain Thomas Procter, was issued in 1578. One of the chief contributors was Owen Roydon, who may have been a brother of Matthew Roydon (the friend of Chapman and author of a famous elegy on Sir Philip Sidney). Many of the poems are of a sententious character and are written in long cumbersome metres; but there are also some sprightly love-ditties.

Fourth on the list comes Clement Robinson's *Handful of Pleasant Delights,* 1584, a very choice collection. Here first appeared the delightful ballad of *Lady Greensleeves;* here we may read the " proper song " beginning—

> " Fain would I have a pretty thing
>   To give unto my lady ;
> I name no thing, nor I mean no thing,
>   But as pretty a thing as may be," &c. ;

and here is the wooing-song (to the tune of " The
Marchaunt's Daughter went over the field ")—

> " Maid, will ye love me, yea or no?
> Tell me the truth and let me go.
> It can be no less than a sinful deed,
> Trust me truly,
> To linger a lover that looks to speed ,
> In due time duly," &c.

" L. G.," " I. P.," " I. Tomson," and " Peter
Picks," were among the contributors ; all four
are unknown, and " Peter Picks " is doubtless a
pseudonym.

Antony Munday's *A Banquet of Dainty Conceits*, 1588, of which only a single copy is known,[1]
must not be classed with the anthologies ; for
the twenty-two pieces which it contains were all
written by Munday. Intrinsically the poems
have little interest ; but the collection is on that
account important, as affording excellent proof
that Antony Munday was not the " Shepherd
Tony " of *England's Helicon.* Munday was an
inferior writer, whose pen was chiefly employed
in composing city-pageants and translating
romances from the French. Among these
Dainty Conceits there is not even a passable
lyric to be found. As a specimen of the general

[1] The possessor of this unique book is Mr. Alfred H.
Huth, who very kindly allowed me to examine it.

poverty of the collection the following stanza may be quoted :—

> " Soft fire makes sweet malt, they say ;
> Few words well placed the wise will weigh ;
> Time idle spent in trifles vain
> Returns no guerdon for thy pain ;
> But time well spent doth profit bring,
> And of good works will honour spring.
> Bestow thy time then in such sort
> That virtue may thy deeds support ;
> The greater profit thou shalt see,
> And better fame will go of thee."

Very thin gruel this ; and there are eight more stanzas. After reading these *Dainty Conceits* I shall stubbornly refuse to believe that Munday could have written any of the poems attributed in *England's Helicon* to the Shepherd Tony.

In 1593 appeared the fifth anthology, *The Phœnix Nest*, edited by "R. S. of the Inner Temple, Gentleman." To whom the initials "R. S." belong is a mystery ; but all lovers of poetry are indebted to the taste and zeal of this unknown editor. Among the known contributors were Thomas Lodge and Nicholas Breton ; and there are many exquisite poems by anonymous writers.

England's Helicon, first published in 1600 and republished with additions in 1614, stands sixth on the list. *England's Parnassus*, 1600, and *Belvedere*, 1600, I omit ; for they are dictionaries of poetical quotations rather than anthologies. The last anthology (the seventh) published in Elizabeth's reign was Francis Davison's *Poetical Rhapsody*, a collection of the highest interest, first printed in 1602 ; reprinted with additions in 1608 ; again, with many additions, in 1611 ; and for the fourth time (with a new arrangement of the poems) in 1621.

The reader will find in *England's Helicon* some of the sweetest lyrical and pastoral poetry of the Elizabethan age, dainty little masterpieces by Lodge, Breton, Greene, Barnfield, and many other true-born poets. He will also find, I regret to say, two dozen poems by Bartholomew Young (or Yong), translator of Montemayor's *Diana*. It would be a relief to me if I could oust Young's verses from this anthology ; but, as that course would be unscholarly, I must content myself with issuing a prefatory *caveat* to unwary readers. Possibly Bartholomew Young (an unpoetical name) may even find here and there an admirer ; but in my judgment he seldom rises above, and not seldom falls below, mediocrity. The selections are made for the most part with such excellent taste that the constant occurrence of Young's name can only be explained on the assumption that he was a close friend of the indulgent editor.

Who was the editor ? Clearly "A. B." (who-

ever he may have been), author of the prefatory
sonnet " To his loving kind friend Master
John Bodenham." Yet bibliographers, one after
another, with remarkable perversity, assure us
that Bodenham was the editor. As I have
elsewhere[1] shown, Bodenham did not edit
any of the Elizabethan miscellanies attributed
to him by bibliographers ; he projected their
publication and he befriended the editors. The
miscellanies issued under his patronage were
(1) *Wit's Commonwealth,* 1597, (2) *Wit's
Theatre,* 1598,—popular collections (which
passed through many editions) of brief extracts
from philosophers, orators, fathers of the Church,
&c. ; (3) *Belvedere or the Garden of the Muses,*
1600, ed. 2, 1610, a collection of scrappy poetical
quotations seldom exceeding a couplet in length ;
(4) *England's Helicon.* On turning to the
epistle of Nicholas Ling the publisher, prefixed
to (1) *Wit's Commonwealth,* we find that Ling
collected the material for that volume and that
Bodenham merely suggested the publication of
such a collection. In regard to (2) *Wit's Theatre,*
it is perfectly clear that Robert Allott[2] was the

---

[1] *Dictionary of National Biography :* articles on *Allott,
Robert,* and *Bodenham, John.*

[2] Allott was also the editor of *England's Parnassus,*
for in a copy which belonged to Farmer, and which is
now in the British Museum (pressmark 238. b. 24), his

editor ; for a copy (preserved in the British Museum) of the 1599 edition contains an epistle in which Allott dedicates to Bodenham this " collection of the flowers of antiquities and histories." Prefixed to (3) *Belvedere* is a sonnet by A[ntony ?] M[unday ?] in which Bodenham is addressed as

> "Art's Lover, Learning's friend,
> First causer and collector of these flowers,"—

words which imply that Bodenham had suggested the compilation and had prepared some materials for the volume. Bodenham gave his support and patronage ; Ling, Allott, and "A. B." collected and arranged the materials for the miscellanies with which Bodenham's name is associated.

The second edition of *England's Helicon*, 1614, which contains nine additional poems, has a dedicatory sonnet by the publisher, Richard More, addressed "To the truly virtuous and honourable Lady, the Lady Elizabeth Carey." This lady was, I suppose, the wife of Sir Henry Carey (created Lord Falkland in 1610), and mother of the famous Lucius Lord Falkland who fell at Newbury. She was certainly the " Lady E[lizabeth] C[arey]" who wrote

name is printed at full length below the dedicatory sonnet addressed to Sir William Mounson.

The Tragedy of Mariam the Fair Queen of Jewry, 1613. John Davies of Hereford in 1612 linked her name with the names of Lucy Countess of Bedford and Mary Countess-Dowager of Pembroke in the dedicatory verse-epistle[1] prefixed to his *Muse's Sacrifice;* and to her in 1633 William Sheares the publisher dedicated the collective edition of Marston's plays. She died in 1639.

Now let us turn to the contents of *England's Helicon.*

Page 17. *The Shepherd to his Chosen Nymph.* This poem is from Sidney's *Astrophel and Stella*, which passed through three editions in 1591; and it evidently refers to some real incident, of which we have no knowledge.

Page 19. *Theorello.* The initials "E. B." doubtless belong to Edmund Bolton, whose signature is subscribed at full length to the

---

[1] Davies makes it perfectly clear that his patroness wrote *Mariam:*—

"Thou mak'st Melpomen proud and my heart great
　Of such a pupil who, in buskin fine,
With feet of state dost make thy Muse to meet
　The scenes of Syracuse and Palestine."

The authorship of that play has been a puzzle to bibliographers, for there were at least three famous ladies who bore the title of Lady Elizabeth Carey (or Carew), poem on pp. 34-5. Bolton, one of the most learned men of his time, was the author of the *Elements of Armories*, 1610, and an interesting treatise *Hypercritica*, circ. 1618, first published by Antony Hall at the end of *Triveti Annales*, 1722. He was a retainer of George Villiers Duke of Buckingham, and accompanied him on his memorable journey to Spain in 1623 (*Collectanea*, Oxford Historical Society, i. 278). He was one of those who laboured to establish a Royal Academy or College of Honour "for the breeding and bringing up of the nobility and gentry of this kingdom,"—a scheme which was frequently discussed but never got beyond the stage of discussion. Bolton died about the year 1633.

There are three other poems signed " E. B."; and I suppose that they also belong to Bolton.

Page 23. *Astrophel's Love is Dead.* This poem was probably written on the occasion of Stella's (Lady Penelope Devereux') marriage to Lord Rich.

Page 28. *Hobbinol's Ditty.* From the Fourth Æglogue of Spenser's *Shepheardes Calender*.

Page 32. *The Shepherd's Daffodil.* From Michael Drayton's *Ninth Eclogue*, first published in *Poems Lyric and Heroic*, 8vo. (1605?), and republished in the collective edition of Drayton's works, 1619, fol. I have included it in my *Selections from the Poetry of Michael Drayton* (privately printed, 1883). In Drayton's works it is printed in the form of a dialogue between Batte and Gorbo.

Page 35. *Melicertus' Madrigal.* From Robert Greene's *Menaphon. Camilla's Alarum to Slumbering Euphues,* &c., 1589, 4to.

Page 36. *Old Damon's Pastoral.* This poem of Lodge seems to have been published for the first time in *England's Helicon.*

Page 38. *Perigot and Cuddie's Roundelay.* From the Eighth Æglogue of Spenser's *Shepheardes Calender.*

Page 40. *Phyllida and Corydon.* First printed in *The Honourable Entertainment given to the Queen's Majesty in Progress at Elvetham in Hampshire, by the Right Honourable the Earl of Hertford,* 1591, under the title of "The Ploughman's Song." It is set to music in Michael Este's *Madrigals,* 1604, and in Henry Youll's *Canzonets,* 1608.

Page 41. *To Colin Clout.* This charming lyric was written by "The Shepherd Tony," who contributed six other poems It would be pleasant to be able to identify the Shepherd Tony; but I fear that he will remain a mere *nominis umbra.* The suggestion that the delightful lyrist was Antony Copley, author of *A Fig for Fortune,* 1596, and *Wits, Fits, and*

Fancies, 1614, is ridiculous ; and equally ridiculous is the suggestion that he was Antony Munday.

Page 42. *Rowland's Song in Praise of the Fairest Beta.* This poem was first published in Michael Drayton's *Idea, the Shepherd's Garland*, 1593, and was republished, with some textual variations, for Drayton was constantly altering his poems, in *Poems Lyric and Heroic* (1605?).

Page 46. *The Barginet of Antimachus.* As I cannot find this poem among Lodge's works (collected by the Hunterian Club), I suppose that it first appeared in *England's Helicon*.

Page 48. *Menaphon's Roundelay.* From Greene's *Menaphon*, 1589. The quiet beauty of the opening lines will appeal to every reader.

Page 49. *A Pastoral of Phyllis and Corydon.* From Nicholas Breton's *The Arbor of Amorous Devices*, 1597, of which only one copy (and that imperfect) is preserved—in the Capell Collection at Trinity College, Cambridge. Breton's works (with the exception of some unique volumes in private hands) were collected by Dr. Grosart in 1879, two vols. 4to.

Page 50. *Corydon and Melampus' Song.* From George Peele's pastoral *The Hunting of Cupid*, of which fragments are extant among the Drummond MSS.

Pages 51-53. *Tityrus to his fair Phyllis;*

b

[*Love's Thrall*]; *Another by the same author.*
The first of these three poems is signed "I. D.";
the second and third are signed "I. M." It has
been supposed that "I. D." is Sir John Davies,
among whose works Dr. Grosart prints the
first poem. In an old MS. list (presumed to be
in the writing of Francis Davison, editor of the
Poetical Rhapsody,) of the contributors to
England's Helicon, preserved in Harl. MS. 280,
we find instead of "I. D." the signature "I.
Dauis." Put not your faith in manuscripts.
The poems, all three, were written by John
Dickenson, and are found in *The Shepherd's
Complaint*, n. d. (circ. 1594), of which a copy
was discovered some few years ago (by Mr.
Charles Edmonds) in a lumber room at Lam-
port Hall, Northamptonshire, the seat of Sir
Charles Isham, Bart. I hope the reader will be
duly grateful to me for clearing up a difficulty
which has sorely vexed the souls of previous
inquirers. Some stiffly declared that "I. M."
was John Marston (save the mark!), others
voted for Jervase Markham; and the great
Dean of St. Paul's, John Donne, was brought
into the lists to dispute Sir John Davies' claim
to the initials "I. D."

Page 53. *Menaphon to Persana.* From
Robert Greene's *Menaphon*, 1589.

Page 54. *A Sweet Pastoral.* I cannot find

this poem among those works of Breton which Dr. Grosart has printed. It is perhaps in *The Bower of Delights* (jealously guarded at Britwell).

Page 56. *Harpalus' Complaint.* This poem (here ascribed to the Earl of Surrey) was first printed among *Poems by Uncertain Authors* in *Tottel's Miscellany,* 1557.

Page 63. *The Nymphs meeting their May-Queen.* This poem of Watson (who has been greatly overpraised by some modern critics) seems to have been addressed to Queen Elizabeth ; and I suspect that it formed part of some (lost ?) *Entertainment.* It is set to music in Francis Pilkington's *First Book of Songs or Airs,* 1605.

Page 64. *Colin Clout's Mournful Ditty.* Introductory stanzas to Spenser's *Astrophel, a pastorall Elegie . upon the Death of Sir Philip Sidney.*

Page 65. *Damætas' Jig.* The author, John Wootton, is supposed by Brydges to be Sir John Wotton (half-brother of Sir Henry Wotton), third son of Thomas Wotton of Bocton Malherb, in Kent, by Elizabeth his first wife, daughter of Sir John Rudstone, knight. Izaak Walton describes Sir John as "a gentleman excellently accomplished both by learning and travel, who was knighted by Queen Elizabeth, and looked

upon with more than ordinary favour and with
intentions of preferment; but Death in his
younger years put a period to his growing
hopes."

Page 66. *Montanus' Praise of his fair Phœbe.*
From Lodge's romance *Rosalind, Euphues'
Golden Legacy,* first printed in 1590.

Page 67. *Complaint of Thestilis.* This poem,
here ascribed to the Earl of Surrey, was first
printed among *Poems of Uncertain Authors*
in *Tottel's Miscellany,* 1557.

Page 69. *To Phyllis the fair Shepherdess.*
This poem is signed " S. E. D." (*i.e.* Sir Edward
Dyer, to whom it is attributed in Davison's
Harleian MS. list); but there can be little doubt
that it belongs to Lodge, for it is found in his
Phillis, 1593.

Page 70. *The Shepherd Doron's Jig.* From
Robert Greene's *Menaphon,* 1589.

Page 71. *Astrophel's Song of Phyllida and
Corydon.* This poem of Breton was originally
signed " S. Phil. Sidney" in ed. 1600, but a slip
was inserted with the signature " N. Breton."
It appears to have been printed for the first
time in *England's Helicon;* and the same re-
mark applies to other poems of Breton in this
collection.

Page 74. *The Passionate Shepherd's Song.*
Printed in *Love's Labour Lost,* 1598. It is

the second of the *Sonnets to sundry notes
of Music,* appended to *The Passionate Pilgrim by W. Shakespeare,* 1599 (printed by W.
Jaggard).

Page 75. *The Unknown Shepherd's Complaint.*
From the *Sonnets* appended to *The Passionate
Pilgrim,* 1599. It had previously appeared, set
to music, in Thomas Weelkes' *Madrigals,* 1597,
without an author's name. An early MS. copy
(also without author's name) is preserved in
Harl. MS. 6910, fol. 156. There is good ground
for attributing the poem (which is signed *Ignoto*
in *England's Helicon*) to Richard Barnfield ; for
the poem that follows, which undoubtedly belongs to Barnfield, is headed " Another of *the
same Shepherd's.*"

Page 76. *Another of the same Shepherd's.*
These verses are from a poem of Richard Barnfield printed among *Poems in divers Humours*
appended to the *Encomion of Lady Pecunia,*
1598. The editor of *England's Helicon* trun-
cated Barnfield's poem, adding two lines of his
own to the portion he adopted—

> " Even so, poor bird, like thee
> None alive will pity me."

In the *Sonnets* appended to *The Passionate
Pilgrim,* 1599, the poem is printed *in extenso.*

Page 77. *The Shepherd's Allusion,* &c. From
Watson's *Hecatompathia,* 1582.

Page 78. *Montanus' Sonnet.* From Lodge's *Rosalind*, 1590.

Page 79. *Phœbe's Sonnet.* Also from Lodge's *Rosalind.*

Page 84. *Doron's Description of his fair Shepherdess Samela.* From Greene's *Menaphon,* 1589.

Page 85. *Wodenfride's Song.* It has been suggested (by Ritson) that the initials " W. H." belong to William Hunnis, a contributor to *The Paradise of Dainty Devices* and author of some devotional poems ; but both this poem and the next have more merit than any of Hunnis' authentic productions.

Page 90. *Phyllida's Love-Call.* This exquisite poem, signed *Ignoto,* has been ascribed, without the slightest authority, to Sir Walter Raleigh.

Page 93. *The Shepherd's Solace.* From Watson's *Hecatompathia.*

Page 93. *Syrenus' Song to his Eugerius.* The poems of Bartholomew Young (of which there are far too many in this collection) are taken from his translation, published in 1598, but finished in MS. May 1st, 1583, of Montemayor's *Diana,* a famous Spanish romance.

Page 100. *The Shepherd's Ode.* First published in Richard Barnfield's *Cynthia,* 1595.

Page 103. *The Shepherd's Commendation of his Nymph.* This poem of Edward Vere, Earl of Oxford, had already appeared in *The Phœnix Nest,* 1593. The Earl of Oxford was also a contributor to *The Paradise of Dainty Devices.* His poems have been collected by Dr. Grosart.

Page 105. *Corydon to his Phyllis.* This poem, here ascribed to Sir Edward Dyer, had appeared (without the author's name) in *The Phœnix Nest,* 1593.

Page 106. *The Shepherd's Description of Love.* In ed. 1600 of *England's Helicon* this poem was originally subscribed " S. W. R." (*i.e.* Sir Walter Raleigh), but, in the extant copies, over this signature is pasted a slip on which is printed "Ignoto." In Davison's MS. list it is signed " Sir W. Rawley." The poem had been printed, with no distinction of dialogue, and the first line running " Now, what is Love, I pray thee tell ?" in *The Phœnix Nest,* 1593. There is an early MS. copy in Harl. MS. 6910. It was set to music in Robert Jones' *Second Book of Songs and Airs,* 1601.

Page 107. *To his Flocks.* The initials " H. C." doubtless belong to Henry Constable.

Page 108. *A Roundelay between two Shepherds.* This poem of Michael Drayton seems to have been first published in *England's Helicon.* At least I have not succeeded in finding it among his multitudinous works.

Page 109. *The Solitary Shepherd's Song.*

From Lodge's romance *A Margarite of America*, 1596.

Page 110. *The Shepherd's Resolution in Love.* From Watson's *Hecatompathia*.

Page 111. *Corydon's Hymn.* It has been suggested that the initials " T. B." may belong to Thomas Bastard the epigrammatist, author of *Chrestoleros*, 1598.

Page 115. *Corin's Dream of his fair Chloris.* This poem, signed " W. S.," is from William Smith's *Chloris, or the Complaint of the passionate despised Shepherd*, 1596, which has been reprinted in Dr. Grosart's *Occasional Issues.*

Page 116. *The Shepherd Damon's Passion.* From Lodge's *Phillis*, 1593.

Page 117. *The Shepherd Musidorus his Complaint.* From Sidney's *Arcadia*, 1590, p. 77.

Page 117. *The Shepherd's Brawl.* From Sidney's *Arcadia*, 1590, p. 85.

Page 118. *Dorus his Comparisons.* From Sidney's *Arcadia*, 1590, p. 111.

Page 122. *Damelus' Song to his Diaphenia.* By H[enry] C[onstable]. It is set to music in Francis Pilkington's *First Book of Songs or Airs*, 1605.

Page 122. *The Shepherd Eurymachus to his fair Shepherdess Mirimida.* From Robert Greene's *Francesco's Fortunes, or the Second Part of Greene's Never Too Late*, 1590.

Page 127. *The Shepherd's Praise of his sacred Diana.* In ed. 1600 this poem was originally subscribed with the initials "S. W. R." (Sir Walter Raleigh), but over the signature in the extant copies is pasted a slip on which is printed "Ignoto"; and in ed. 1614 the poem is subscribed "Ignoto." It had been printed (without a signature) in *The Phœnix Nest,* 1593. In Davison's Harleian list it is marked "W. R."

Page 128. *The Shepherd's Dump.* This poem, here assigned to S[ir] E[dward] D[yer], is reprinted (with some variations) on p. 239, where it is subscribed "Ignoto." It had already been printed in *The Phœnix Nest,* 1593, where it is attributed to "T. L., Gent." (*i.e.* Thomas Lodge).

Page 131. *Rowland's Madrigal.* This poem of Michael Drayton seems to have been printed for the first time in *England's Helicon.*

Page 135. *Montana the Shepherd, his Love to Aminta.* There is an early copy (with no author's name) of this poem of the Shepherd Tony in Harl. MS. 6910.

Page 136. *The Shepherd's Sorrow for his Phœbe's Disdain.* In ed. 1600 this poem was originally given to "M. F. G." (*i.e.* Mr. Fulke Greville), but over this signature is pasted a slip lettered "Ignoto"; in ed. 1614 the poem is subscribed "I. F." In Davison's MS. list the poem is given to "F. Grevill."

Page 138. *Espilus and Therion their Conten-tion.* From Sidney's masque *The Lady of the May*, first published with the poems appended to the 1598 edition of *Arcadia.*

Page 139. *Old Melibœus' Song.* In ed. 1600 this poem was originally subscribed " M. F. G." (*i.e.* Mr. Fulke Greville); but in the extant copies of ed. 1 a slip (lettered " Ignoto ") is pasted over the signature, and in ed. 1614 there is no signature. The poem is given to " F. Grevill " in Davison's MS. list.

Page 141. *Corydon's Song.* From Lodge's *Rosalind,* 1590.

Page 142. *The Shepherd's Sonnet.* From Richard Barnfield's *Cynthia,* 1595.

Page 145. *Montanus his Madrigal.* From Robert Greene's *Francesco's Fortunes, or the Second Part of Greene's Never Too Late,* 1590.

Page 147. *Astrophel to Stella.* From Sidney's *Astrophel and Stella,* 1591.

Page 153. *Apollo's Love-Song for Fair Daphne.* This poem is set to music in John Dowland's *A Pilgrim's Solace,* 1612. In the last line but one Dowland gives—

" Then this be sure, since it is true perfection."

Page 156. *Amyntas for his Phyllis.* This poem of Watson had appeared in *The Phœnix Nest,* 1593, where it is subscribed " T. W."

Page 160. *Sireno, a Shepherd,* &c.   First printed among the sonnets appended to the 1598 edition of Sidney's *Arcadia.*

Page 169. *Philistus' Farewell to False Clorinda.* From Thomas Morley's *Madrigals to Four Voices.. The First Book,* 1594.

Page 169. *Rosalind's Madrigal.*   From Lodge's *Rosalind,* 1590.

Page 172. *Montanus' Sonnet.*   This poem, though it is ascribed to S[ir] E[dward] D[yer] in *England's Helicon,* really belongs to Lodge. It is printed in Lodge's *Rosalind,* 1590.

Page 174. *The Herdman's Happy Life.*   From William Byrd's *Psalms, Sonnets, and Songs,* 1588.

Page 178. *The Shepherd to the Flowers.*   This poem (subscribed "Ignoto") was first printed in *The Phœnix Nest,* 1593, with no signature attached.   It is printed in the Oxford edition of Raleigh's poems, and in Hannah's *Poems by Raleigh, Wotton,* &c.; but Raleigh's claim to the authorship is without foundation.

Page 186. *To Amaryllis.*   From William Byrd's *Psalms, Sonnets, and Songs,* 1588.

Page 190. *Of Phyllida.*   From William Byrd's *Psalms, Sonnets, and Songs,* 1588.

Page 194. *Philon the Shepherd his Song.* From William Byrd's *Songs of sundry Natures,* 1589.

Page 195. *Lycoris the Nymph, her Sad Song.* From Thomas Morley's *Madrigals to Four Voices,* 1594.

Page 196. *To his Flocks.* From John Dowland's *First Book of Songs or Airs,* 1597.

Page 196. *To his Love.* From the same songbook of Dowland's.

Page 198. *Another of his Cynthia.* From the same song-book of Dowland's. This poem was doubtless written by Fulke Greville, Lord Brooke; for it is not only ascribed to him in Davison's MS. list, but is printed in *Certain learned and elegant works of the Right Honourable Fulke, Lord Brooke,* 1633, fol.

Page 199. *Another to his Cynthia.* From the same song-book. In Davison's MS. list this poem is ascribed to the Earl of Cumberland.

Page 200. *Montanus' Sonnet in the Woods.* Though this poem is attributed in *England's Helicon* to S[ir] E[dward] D[yer], it really belongs to Lodge, and is found in *Rosalind,* 1590.

Page 201. *The Shepherd's Sorrow, being disdained in Love.* From Lodge's *Phillis,* 1593; it is also found in *The Phœnix Nest,* 1593.

Page 204. *A Pastoral Song between Phyllis and Amaryllis.* By H[enry] C[onstable].

Page 206. *The Shepherd's Anthem.* This poem does not appear in the 1593 collection of

Michael Drayton's eclogues *Idea, the Shepherd's Garland*, but it is found in the second eclogue of *Poems Lyric and Pastoral* (1605 ?).

Page 209. *Another of Astrophel.* From the poems appended to the 1598 edition of Sidney's *Arcadia.*

Page 210. *An Invective against Love.* This poem was added in ed. 1614, and in the prefatory table bears the signature " Ignoto." It had been previously printed in Davison's *Rhapsody*, 1602, where it is subscribed " A. W." There are many charming poems by " A. W." in Davison's collection, but it is unknown to whom the initials belong. In Harl. MS. 280 is a long list (presumed to be in the handwriting of Francis Davison) of all the poems written by " A. W." I reserve my comments on that list for another occasion. The document is very important, and I hope to examine it at considerable length.

Page 212. *Fair Phyllis to her Shepherd.* Ritson's suggestion that the signature " J. G." may belong to John Gough, a dramatist of Charles I.'s day (author of *The Strange Discovery*, 1640), is very wide of the mark, unworthy of so acute a scholar as Ritson. Brydges urges the claim of John Grange, author of the *Golden Aphroditis*, 1577 ; but there is little to be said in Grange's favour. The verses are very much in Constable's manner.

Page 215. *The Shepherd's Song of Venus and Adonis.* By H[enry] C[onstable].

Page 220. *Thyrsis the Shepherd, his Death Song.* From N. Yonge's *Musica Transalpina,* 1588. The two following pieces are from the same song-book.

Page 222. *The Shepherd's Slumber.* Signed *Ignoto* in ed. 1600 ; there is no signature in ed. 1614. It has been ascribed, without evidence, to Raleigh.

Page 226. *If Love be life I long to die.* Added in ed. 1614, where it is subscribed " Ignoto."

Page 227. *Another Sonnet.* This sonnet of Sidney is among the poems appended to the 1598 edition of *Arcadia ;* but it had been previously printed in Constable's *Diana,* &c., 1584.

Page 228. *Of Disdainful Daphne.* " M. H. Nowell" is the signature attached to this poem in ed. 1600 ; "M. N. Howell" in ed. 1614. In Davison's MS. list the poem is given to " H. Nowell." Of the writer, whether his name be Howell or Nowell, nothing is known.

Page 231. *The Nymph's Reply to the Shepherd.* In ed. 1600 this poem was originally sub-scribed " S. W. R." (*i.e.* Sir Walter Raleigh), but over these initials in the extant copies is pasted a slip, on which is printed " Ignoto." It is ascribed to Raleigh by Izaak Walton in *The Compleat Angler,* 1653.

Page 234. *Two Pastorals upon Three Friends Meeting.* This poem of Sidney had already appeared in Davison's *Poetical Rhapsody,* 1602. It is the first of *Two Pastorals made by Sir Philip Sidney upon his meeting with his two worthy and fellow-poets, Sir Edward Dyer and M. Fulke Greville.* In *England's Helicon* only one of the poems is given, though the title *Two Pastorals* is retained. (The initials in the right-hand margin of the fifth stanza belong, of course, to the three poets.)

Page 240. *An Heroical Poem.* This poem had previously appeared in Davison's *Poetical Rhapsody,* subscribed "A. W.," and headed "Upon an Heroical Poem which he had begun (in imitation of Virgil) of the first inhabiting of this famous isle by Brute and the Trojans." It is in the Oxford edition of Raleigh's Poems; but there is not the slightest evidence to show that Raleigh was the author. There is an early MS. copy in Harleian MS. 6910 without a signature.

Page 242. *An Excellent Sonnet of a Nymph.* This poem of Sidney seems to have been first printed in *England's Helicon.*

Page 244. *The Lover's Absence kills me,* &c. Printed in Davison's *Poetical Rhapsody,* 1602, with the signature "A. W."

Page 245. *The Shepherd's Conceit of Prometheus.* This sonnet of Dyer, with Sidney's accompanying sonnet, had appeared among the poems appended to the 1598 edition of *Arcadia.*

Page 250. *Love the only price of Love.* Printed in Davison's *Poetical Rhapsody,* 1602, where it is subscribed " A. W."

Page 251. *Colin, the enamoured Shepherd,* &c. This poem and the next are from George Peele's pastoral play, *The Arraignment of Paris,* 1584.

Page 252. *The Shepherds' Consort.* From Thomas Morley's *Madrigals to Four Voices,* 1594.

Page 253. *Thyrsis' Praise of his Mistress.* This poem of William Browne, author of *Britannia's Pastorals,* was first published in *England's Helicon,* ed. 1614.

Page 254. *A Defiance to Disdainful Love.* Printed in Davison's *Poetical Rhapsody,* where it bears the signature "A. W." It is set to music in Robert Jones' *Ultimum Vale* [1608].

Page 255. *An Epithalamium.* Printed for the first time in *England's Helicon,* 1614. The writer, Christopher Brooke, joined William Browne and George Wither in writing *The Shepherd's Pipe,* 1614. He is the author of a rare poem, *The Ghost of Richard III.* There is a MS. copy of the *Epithalamium* in the Bodleian Library.

From the foregoing notes it will be seen that, with few exceptions, the poems in *England's Helicon* can be identified. Reader, I will not longer detain you from the banquet.

INDEX OF FIRST LINES.

ENGLANDS

HELICON.

Casta placent superis,
  pura cum veste venite,
Et manibus puris
  sumite fontis aquam.

AT LONDON

Printed by I. R. for *Iohn Flasket*, and are
to be sold in Paules Church-yard, at the signe
of the Beare. 1600.

TO HIS LOVING KIND FRIEND,
MASTER JOHN BODENHAM.[1]

WIT'S Commonwealth, the first-fruits of thy pains,
   Drew on *Wit's Theatre*, thy second son :
By both of which I cannot count the gains
And wondrous profit that the world hath won.
Next, in the *Muses' Garden* gathering flowers,
Thou mad'st a nosegay as was never sweeter :
Whose scent will savour to Time's latest hours ;
And for the greatest Prince no posy meeter.
Now comes thy *Helicon*, to make complete
And furnish up thy last imposed design :
My pains herein, I cannot term it great,
But whatsoe'er, my love (and all) is thine.
   Take love, take pains, take all remains in me :
   And where thou art, my heart still lives with thee.
A. B.

---

[1] Concerning Bodenham, and this prefatory sonnet, see *Introduction.*

TO HIS VERY LOVING FRIENDS,
M. NICHOLAS WANTON AND
M. GEORGE FAUCET.

THOUGH many miles (but more occasions) do sunder us (kind Gentlemen) yet a promise at parting doth in justice claim performance, and assurance of gentle acceptance would mightily condemn me if I should neglect it. *Helicon*, though not as I could wish, yet in such good sort as time would permit, having past the pikes of the press, comes now to York to salute her rightful Patron first, and next (as his dear friends and kinsmen) to offer you her kind service. If she speed well there, it is all she requires ; if they frown at her here, she greatly not cares: for the wise (she knows) will never be other than themselves : as for such then as would seem so, but neither are, nor ever will be, she holds this as a main principle, —that their malice need as little be feared, as their favour or friendship is to be desired. So hoping you will not forget us there, as we continually shall be mindful of you here, I leave you to the delight of *England's Helicon*.

Yours in all he may,

A. B.

TO THE READER, IF INDIFFERENT.

MANY honoured names have heretofore (in their particular interest) patronized some part of these inventions: many here be, that only these Collections have brought to light, and not inferior (in the best opinions) to any before published. The travail that hath been taken in gathering them from so many hands, hath wearied some hours, which severed, might in part have perished; digested into this mean volume, may in the opinion of some not be altogether unworthy the labour. If any man hath been defrauded of any thing by him composed, by another man's title put to the same, he hath this benefit by this collection, freely to challenge his own in public, where else he might be robbed of his proper due. No one thing being here placed by the Collector of the same under any man's name, either at large, or in letters, but as it was delivered by some especial copy coming to his hands. No one man, that shall take offence that his name is published to any invention of his, but he shall within the reading of a leaf or two, meet with another in reputation every way equal with himself, whose name hath been before printed to his poem, which now taken away were more than theft: which may satisfy him that would fain seem curious, or be entreated for his fame.

Now, if any stationer shall find fault that his copies are robbed by any thing in this Collection, let me ask him this question :—Why more in this, than in any divine or human author? from whence a man (writing of that argument) shall gather any saying, sentence, simile, or example, his name put to it who is the author of the same. This is the simplest of many reasons that I could urge, though perhaps the nearest his capacity, but that I would be loth to trouble myself to satisfy him. Further, if any man whatsoever, in prizing of his own birth or fortune, shall take in scorn that a far meaner man in the eye of the world shall be placed by him, I tell him plainly, whatsoever so excepting, that that man's wit is set by his, not that man by him. In which degree, the names of poets (all fear and duty ascribed to her great and sacred name) have been placed with the names of the greatest princes of the world, by the most authentic and worthiest judgments, without disparagement to their sovereign titles : which if any man taking exception thereat, in ignorance know not, I hold him unworthy to be placed by the meanest that is but graced with the title of a poet. Thus, gentle reader, I wish thee all happiness.

L. N.[1]

---

[1] The transposed initials of Nicholas Ling, a well-known Elizabethan publisher.

ENGLANDS

HELICON.

OR

THE MVSES

HARMONY.

The Courts of Kings heare no such straines,
As daily lull the Rusticke Swaines.

LONDON:

Printed for RICHARD MORE, and are to
be sould at his Shop in S. Dunstanes
Church-yard. 1614.

TO THE TRULY VIRTUOUS AND
HONOURABLE LADY, THE LADY
ELIZABETH CAREY.

DEIGN, worthy Lady, (England's happy Muse,
    Learning's delight, that all things else exceeds,)
To shield from envy's paw and time's abuse
The tuneful notes of these our shepherds' reeds.

Sweet is the concord, and the music such
That at it rivers have been seen to dance ;
When these musicians did their sweet pipes touch,
In silence lay the vales as in a trance.

The Satyr stopped his race to hear them sing,
And bright Apollo to these lays hath given
So great a gift, that any favouring
The shepherd's quill shall with the lights of heaven

    Have equal fate : then cherish these (fair stem) ;
    So shall they live by thee, and thou by them.

      Your honour's

        ever to command,

            RICHARD MORE.

THE TABLE OF ALL THE SONGS AND PASTORALS, WITH THE AUTHORS' NAMES, CONTAINED IN THIS BOOK.

FINIS.

THE SHEPHERD TO HIS CHOSEN
NYMPH.

ONLY joy, now here you are,
　　Fit to hear and ease my care ;
Let my whisp'ring voice obtain
Sweet reward for sharpest pain ;
　　Take me to thee, and thee to me :—
　　" No, no, no, no, my dear, let be !"

Night hath closed all in her cloak ;
Twinkling stars love-thoughts provoke :
Danger hence good care doth keep ;
Jealousy itself doth sleep ;
　　Take me to thee, and thee to me :—
　　" No, no, no, no, my dear, let be !"

Better place no wit can find
Cupid's yoke to loose or bind ;
These sweet flowers, our[1] fine bed too,
Us in their best language woo ;

---

[1] *England's Helicon* " on."—Where I have altered the text
of Sidney's poems, I am supported by the authority of the 1591
editions of *Astrophel and Stella.*

C

Take me to thee, and thee to me :—
" No, no, no, no, my dear, let be !"

This small light the moon bestows,
Serves thy beams but to disclose,[1]
So to raise my heart[2] more high :
Fear not, else none can us spy ;
Take me to thee, and thee to me :—
" No, no, no, no, my dear, let be !"

That you heard was but a mouse,
Dumb sleep holdeth all the house ;
Yet asleep methinks they say,
Young folks, take time while you may ;
Take me to thee, and thee to me :—
" No, no, no, no, my dear, let be !"

Niggard Time threats, if we miss
This large offer of our bliss,
Long stay ere he grant the same :
Sweet, then, while each thing doth frame,
Take me to thee, and thee to me :—
" No, no, no, no, my dear, let be !"

Your fair mother is abed,
Candles out and curtains spread ;
She thinks you do letters write :
Write, but let me first indite :
Take me to thee, and thee to me :—
" No, no, no, no, my dear, let be !"

[1] *E. H.* " enclose."   [2] *E. H.* " hap."

Sweet (alas !) why strive[1] you thus ?
Concord better fitteth us ;
Leave to Mars the force of hands,
Your power in your beauty stands :
    Take me to thee, and thee to me :—
    " No, no, no, no, my dear, let be !"

Woe to me ! and[2] do you swear
Me to hate, but I forbear ?
Cursèd be my destinies all,
That brought me so[3] high to fall !
    Soon with my death I will please thee :—
    " No, no, no, no, my dear, let be !"
        Finis.   *Sir Phil. Sidney.*

THEORELLO.

A Shepherd's Idillion.

YOU shepherds which on hillocks sit,
    Like princes in their thrones ;
And guide your flocks, which else would flit,
    Your flocks of little ones ;
Good kings have not disdained it,
    But shepherds have been named ;
A sheep-hook is a sceptre fit
    For people well reclaimed.
The shepherd's life so honour'd is and praised
That kings less happy seem, though higher raised.

[1] *E. H.* " saine."   [2] *E. H.* " and you doe."
[3] *E. H.* " to so high a fall."

The summer sun hath gilded fair
    With morning rays the mountains ;
The birds do carol in the air,
    And naked nymphs in fountains ;
The sylvans in their shagged hair,
    With hamadryads trace ;
The shady satyrs make a quire,
    Which rocks with echoes grace.
All breathe delight, all solace in the season :
Not now to sing, were enemy to reason.

Cosma, my love, and more than so,
    The life of my affections,
Nor life alone but lady too,
    And queen of their directions ;
Cosma my love is fair, you know,
    And, which you shepherds know not,
Is (Sophy said) thence called so ;
    But names her beauty show not.
Yet hath the world no better name than she :
And than the world no fairer thing can be.

The sun upon her forehead stands,
    Or jewel sun-like glorious ;
Her forehead wrought with Jove's own hands,
    For heavenly white notorious :
Her golden locks like Hermus' sands,
    (Or than bright Hermus brighter,)
A spangled caul binds in with bands,
    Than silver morning lighter :
And if the planets are the chief in skies,
No other stars than planets are her eyes.

Her cheek, her lip, fresh cheek more fresh
   Than self-blown buds of roses ;
Rare lip, more red than those of flesh,
   Which thousand sweets encloses ;
Sweet breath, which all things doth refresh,
   And words than breath far sweeter :
Cheek firm, lip firm, not frail nor nesh,
   As substance which is fleeter :
In praise do not surmount, although in placing
Her crystal neck, round breasts, and arms embracing.

The thorough-shining air, I ween,
   Is not so perfect clear,
As is the sky of her fair skin,
   Whereon no spots appear.
The parts which ought not to be seen,
   For sovereign worth excel :
Her thighs with azure branched been,
   And all in her are well.
Long ivory hands, legs straighter than the pine,
Well shapen feet, but virtue most divine.

Nor clothed like a shepherdess,
   But rather like a queen ;
Her mantle doth the form express,
   Of all which may be seen.
Robe fitter for an emperess
   Than for a shepherd's love,
Robe fit alone for such a lass
   As emperors doth move.
Robe which heaven's queen, the pride of her own
     brother,
Would grace herself with, or with such another.

Who ever (and who else but Jove?)
    Embroidered the same,
He knew the world, and what did move
    In all the mighty frame.
So well (belike his skill to prove)
    The counterfeits he wrought :
Of wood-gods and of every grove,
    And all which else was ought.
Is there a beast, a bird, a fish worth note ?
Than that he drew and pictured in her coat.

A veil of lawn like vapour thin,
    Unto her ankle trails ;
Through which the shapes discernèd bin
    As to and fro it sails,
Shapes both of men, who never lin
    To search her wonders out,
Of monsters and of gods a-kin
    Which her empale about.
A little world her flowing garment seems :
And who but as a wonder thereof deems ?

For here and there appear forth towers
    Among the chalky downs,
Cities among the country bowers
    Which smiling sunshine crowns :
Her metal buskins deck'd with flowers,
    As th' earth when frosts are gone,
Besprinkled are with orient showers
    Of hail and pebble stone :
Her feature peerless, peerless her attire,
I can but love her love with zeal entire.

Oh ! who can sing her beauties best,
　Or that remains unsung ?
Do thou, Apollo, tune the rest :
　Unworthy is my tongue.
To gaze on her is to be blest,
　So wondrous fair her face is ;
Her fairness cannot be exprest
　In goddesses nor graces.
I love my love, the goodly work of nature :
Admire her face, but more admire her stature.

On thee (O Cosma) will I gaze,
　And read thy beauties ever :
Delighting in the blessed maze,
　Which can be ended never.
For in the lustre of thy rays
　Appears thy parent's brightness :
Who himself infinite displays
　In thee his proper greatness.
My song must end, but never my desire,
For Cosma's face is Theorello's fire.

　　　　　Finis.　　　　*E. B.*

ASTROPHEL'S LOVE IS DEAD.

RING out your bells, let mourning shows be
　　spread,
　　　　For Love is dead !
　　All Love is dead, infected
　　With plague of deep disdain,

Worth as nought worth rejected,
And faith fair scorn doth gain.
From so ungrateful fancy,
From such a female frenzy,
From them that use men thus,
Good Lord deliver us !

Weep, neighbours, weep, do you not hear it said
That Love is dead?
His deathbed peacock's folly,
His winding sheet is shame,
His will false-seeming holy,
His sole exec'tor blame.
From so ungrateful fancy,
From such a female frenzy,
From them that use men thus,
Good Lord deliver us !

Let dirge be sung and trentals richly[1] read,
For Love is dead !
And wrong his tomb ordaineth,
My mistress' marble heart :
Which epitaph containeth,
Her eyes were once his dart.
From so ungrateful fancy,
From such a female frenzy,
From them that use men thus,
Good Lord deliver us !

Alas ! I lie, rage has this error bred,
Love is not dead.

[1] In ed. 1598 of the *Arcadia*, where this poem first appeared,
the reading is "rightly."

Love is not dead but sleepeth
In her unmatchèd mind :
Where she his counsel keepeth,
Tell due desert she find.
   Therefore from so vile fancy,
   To call such wit a frenzy,
  Who Love can temper thus,
     Good Lord deliver us !
           Finis.   *Sir Phil. Sidney.*

A PALINODE.

AS withereth the primrose by the river,
  As fadeth summer's-sun from gliding fountains,
As vanisheth the light-blown bubble ever,
As melteth snow upon the mossy mountains ;
So melts, so vanisheth, so fades, so withers,
The rose, the shine, the bubble, and the snow,
Of praise, pomp, glory, joy (which short life gathers),
Fair praise, vain pomp, sweet glory, brittle joy.
The withered primrose by the mourning river,
The faded summer's-sun from weeping fountains,
The light-blown bubble vanished for ever,
The molten snow upon the naked mountains,
  Are emblems that the treasures we uplay
  Soon wither, vanish, fade, and melt away.

For as the snow, whose lawn did over-spread
Th' ambitious hills, which giant-like did threat

To pierce the heaven with their aspiring head,
Naked and bare doth leave their craggy seat ;
When as the bubble, which did empty fly
The dalliance of the undiscernèd wind,
On whose calm rolling waves it did rely,
Hath shipwreck made, where it did dalliance find ;
And when the sunshine which dissolved the snow,
Coloured the bubble with a pleasant vary,
And made the rathe and timely primrose grow,
Swarth clouds with-drawn (which longer time do tarry)—
  Oh what is praise, pomp, glory, joy, but so
  As shine by fountains, bubbles, flowers, or snow ?

Finis.   *E. B.*

ASTROPHEL THE SHEPHERD, HIS

COMPLAINT TO HIS FLOCK.

GO, my flock, go get ye hence,
      Seek a better place of feeding ;
Where ye may have some defence
    From the storms in my breast breeding,
    And showers from mine eyes proceeding.

Leave a wretch in whom all woe
    Can abide to keep no measure :
Merry flock, such one forego
    Unto whom mirth is displeasure,
    Only rich in mischief's treasure.

Yet (alas !) before you go,
   Hear your woful master's story,
Which to stones I else would show ;
   Sorrow only then hath glory,
   When 'tis excellently sorry.

Stella, fiercest [1] shepherdess,
   Fiercest, but yet fairest ever ;
Stella,[2] whom the heavens still bless,
   Though against me she persever,
   Though I bliss inherit never ;

Stella hath refusèd me,
   Stella, who more love has proved
In this caitiff heart to be,
   Than can in good ewes[3] be moved
   Towards lambkins best beloved.

Stella hath refusèd me ;
   Astrophel, that so well served,
In this pleasant spring must see
   While in pride flowers be preserved,
   Himself only winter-sterved.

Why (alas !) then doth she swear,
   That she loveth me so dearly :
Seeing me so long to bear
   Coals of love that burn so clearly,
   And yet leave me helpless [4] merely ?

---

[1] The 1591 editions of *Astrophel and Stella* read "fairest."
[2] Eds. 1591, "Stella whom O heavens do blesse."
[3] *England's Helicon*, "good by us."
[4] Eds. 1591, "hopelesse."

Is that love? forsooth I trow,
　If I saw my good dog grieved,
And a help for him did know,
　My love should not be believed,
　But he were by me relieved.

No, she hates me, well away!
　Feigning love, somewhat to please me;
Knowing, if she should display
　All her hate, death soon would seize me,
　And of hideous torments ease me.

Then,[1] my dear flock, now adieu!
　But (alas!) if in your straying,
Heavenly Stella meets with you,
　Tell her, in your piteous blaying,
　Her poor slave's unjust decaying.

　　　　　　　Finis.　　*Sir Phil. Sidney.*

HOBBINOL'S DITTY IN PRAISE OF ELIZA,
QUEEN OF THE SHEPHERDS.

YE dainty nymphs that in this blessed brook
　　　Do bathe your breast,
Forsake your watery bowers, and hither look
　　　At my request;
And you, fair virgins that on Parnass dwell,
　Whence floweth Helicon the learnèd well;
　　　Help me to blaze
　　　Her worthy praise,
Who in her sex doth all excel.

[1] Eds. 1591, "Then adieu, deare flocke, adieu."

Of fair Eliza be your silver song,
 That blessèd wight,
The flower of virgins ; may she flourish long
 In princely plight :
For she is Syrinx' daughter, without spot,
Which Pan the shepherds' god on her begot :
 So sprung her grace
 Of heavenly race,
 No mortal blemish may her blot.

See where she sits upon the grassy green,
 O seemly sight !
Yclad in scarlet, like a maiden-queen,
 And ermines white :
Upon her head a crimson coronet,
With daffodils and damask roses set :
 Bay leaves between,
 And primroses green,
 Embellish the sweet violet.

Tell me, have ye beheld her angel's face,
 Like Phœbe fair ?
Her heavenly haviour, her princely grace,
 Can well compare :
The red-rose medled, and the white yfere,
In either cheek depeincten lively cheer.
 Her modest eye,
 Her majesty,
 Where have you seen the like but there ?

I saw Phœbus thrust out his golden head
 On her to gaze :
But when he saw how broad her beams did spread
 It did him maze.

He blush'd to see another sun below,
Ne durst again his fiery face outshow :
    Let him, if he dare,
    His brightness compare
With hers, to have the overthrow.

Show thyself, Cynthia, with thy silver rays,
    And be not abash'd ;
When she the beams of her beauty displays,
    Oh ! how art thou dash'd !
But I'll not match her with Latona's seed ;
Such folly great sorrow to Niobe did breed,
    Now is she a stone,
    And makes deadly moan,
Warning all other to take heed.

Pan may be proud that ever he begot
    Such a Bellibone :
And Syrinx rejoice that ever was her lot
    To bear such a one.
Soon as my younglings cry for the dam,
To her will I offer a milk-white lamb.
    She is my goddess plain,
    And I her shepherd-swain,
Albe for-swonk and for-swat I am.

I see Calliope speed her to the place
    Where my goddess shines :
And after her the other Muses trace
    With their violines.
Bin they not bay-branches, which they do bear,
All for Eliza in her hand to wear ?

So sweetly they play,
And sing all the way,
That it a heaven is to hear.

Lo, how finely the Graces can it foot
To the instrument !
They dancen deftly, and singen soot
In their merriment.
Wants not a fourth Grace to make the dance even?
Let that room to my lady be given.
She shall be a grace
To fill the fourth place,
And reign with the rest in heaven.

And whither runs this bevy of ladies bright,
Ranged in a row?
They been all Ladies of the Lake behight
That unto her go.
Chloris, that is the chief nymph of all,
Of olive-branches bears a coronal.
Olives been for peace,
When wars do surcease,
Such for a princess been principal.

Bring hither the pink and purple columbine,
With gillyflowers;
Bring sweet carnations, and sops-in-wine,
Worn of paramours.
Strew me the ground with daffodowndillies,
And cowslips, and king-cups, and loved lilies.
The pretty paunce
And the chevisaunce
Shall watch with the fair fleur-delice.

Ye shepherd's daughters that dwell on the green,
        Hie you there apace;
Let none come there but such as virgins been,
        To adorn her Grace;
And when you come whereas she is in place,
See that your rudeness do not you disgrace:
        Bind your fillets fast,
        And gird on your waist,
    For more fineness, with a tawdry lace.

Now rise up, Eliza, decked as thou art
        In royal ray:
And now ye dainty damsels may depart
        Each one her way.
I fear I have troubled your troops too long:
Let dame Eliza thank you for her song.
        And if you come hither
        When damsons I gather,
    I will part them all, you among.
                    Finis.   Edm. Spencer.

THE SHEPHERD'S DAFFODIL.

GORBO, as thou cam'st this way
    By yonder little hill,
Or as thou through the fields didst stray,
Saw'st thou my daffodil?

She's in a frock of Lincoln-green,
The colour maids delight;
And never hath her beauty seen
But through a veil of white,

Than roses richer to behold
That dress up lovers' bowers ;
The pansy and the marigold
Are Phœbus' paramours.

Thou well describ'st the daffodil,
It is not full an hour
Since by the spring near yonder hill
I saw that lovely flower.

Yet with my flower thou didst not meet,
Nor news of her dost bring ;
Yet is my daffodil more sweet
Than that by yonder spring.

I saw a shepherd, that doth keep
In yonder field of lilies,
Was making (as he fed his sheep)
A wreath of daffodillies.

Yet, Gorbo, thou delud'st me still,
My flower thou didst not see ;
For know, my pretty daffodil
Is worn of none but me.

To show itself but near her seat
No lily is so bold ;
Except to shade her from the heat,
Or keep her from the cold.

Through yonder vale as I did pass,
Descending from the hill,
I met a smirking bonny lass ;
They call her Daffodil.

D

Whose presence as along she went,
The pretty flowers did greet ;
As though their heads they downward bent
With homage to her feet.

And all the shepherds that were nigh,
From top of every hill,
Unto the valleys loud did cry,
" There goes sweet Daffodil !"

Ay, gentle shepherd, now with joy
Thou all my flock dost fill ;
Come, go with me, thou shepherd's boy,
Let us to Daffodil.

Finis.   Michael Drayton.

A CANZON PASTORAL IN HONOUR OF
HER MAJESTY.

ALAS ! what pleasure, now the pleasant Spring
   Hath given place
To harsh black frosts the sad ground covering,
   Can we, poor we, embrace,
When every bird on every branch can sing,
   Nought but this note of woe, Alas?
Alas ! this note of woe why should we sound?
With us, as May, September hath a prime ;
Then, birds and branches, your Alas is fond,
Which call upon the absent summer-time.
   For did flowers make our May,
   Or the sunbeams your day,

When night and winter did the world embrace,
Well might you wail your ill and sing Alas.

Lo, matron-like the earth herself attires,
    In habit grave ;
Naked the fields are, bloomless are the briars,
    Yet we a summer have,
Who in our clime kindleth these living fires,
    Which blooms can on the briars save.
No ice doth crystallize the running brook,
No blast deflowers the flower-adornèd field.
Crystal is clear, but clearer is the look
Which to our climes these living fires doth yield.
    Winter, though everywhere,
    Hath no abiding here :
On brooks and briars she doth rule alone,
The sun which lights our world is always one.
          Finis.   *Edmund Bolton.*

MELICERTUS' MADRIGAL.

WHAT are my sheep without their wonted food ?
    What is my life except I gain my love?
My sheep consume and faint for want of blood,
My life is lost unless I grace approve.
    No flower that sapless thrives,
    No turtle without fere.

The day, without the sun, doth lower for woe ;
Then woe mine eyes, unless they beauty see !

My sun Samela's eyes, by whom I know
Wherein delight consists, where pleasures be.
    Nought more the heart revives
    Than to embrace his dear.

The stars from earthly humours gain their light,
Our humours by their light possess their power :
Samela's eyes, fed by my weeping sight,
Infuse my pains or joys, by smile or lower.
    So wends the source of love,
    It feeds, it fails, it ends.

Kind looks, clear to your joy, behold her eyes,
Admire her heart, desire to taste her kisses :
In them the heaven of joy and solace lies,
Without them every hope his succour misses.
    Oh, how I live to prove,
    Whereto this solace tends !
           Finis.   *Ro. Greene.*

OLD DAMON'S PASTORAL.

FROM fortune's frowns and change removed,
    Wend, silly flocks, in blessèd feeding :
None of Damon more beloved,
    Feed, gentle lambs, while I sit reading.

Careless worldlings, outrage quelleth
    All the pride and pomp of city,
But true peace with shepherds dwelleth,
    Shepherds who delight in pity.

Whether grace of heaven betideth,
  On our humble minds such pleasure ;
Perfect peace with swains abideth,
  Love and faith is shepherd's treasure.
On the lower plains the thunder
  Little thrives, and nought prevaileth :
Yet in cities breedeth wonder,
  And the highest hills assaileth.

Envy of a foreign tyrant
  Threateneth kings, not shepherds humble ;
Age makes silly swains delirant,
  Thirst of rule [1] gars great men stumble.
What to other seemeth sorry
  Abject state and humble biding,
Is our joy and country glory,
  Highest states have worse betiding :.
Golden cups do harbour poison,
  And the greatest pomp dissembling ;
Court of seasoned words hath foison,
  Treason haunts in most assembling.

Homely breasts do harbour quiet,
  Little fear, and mickle solace :
States suspect their bed and diet,
  Fear and craft do haunt the palace.
Little would I, little want I ;
  Where the mind and store agreeth,
Smallest comfort is not scanty,
  Least he longs that little seeth.
Time hath been that I have longed,
  Foolish I to like of folly,
To converse where honour thronged,
  To my pleasures linkèd wholly.

<hr/>

[1] Ed. 1600, "rules."

Now I see, and seeing sorrow,
  That the day consumed returns not ;
Who dare trust upon to-morrow,
  When nor time nor life sojourns not !
                Finis.   *Thom. Lodge.*

PERIGOT AND CUDDY'S ROUNDELAY.

IT fell upon a holy-eve,
  (Heigho, holy-day !)
When holy fathers wont to shrive
  (Now ginneth this roundelay),
Sitting upon a hill so high,
  (Heigho, the high hill !)
The while my flock did feed thereby,
  The while the shepherd's self did spill ;

I saw the bouncing Bellibone,
  (Heigho, bonny-bell !)
Tripping over the dale alone,
  She can trip it very well ;
Well deckèd in a frock of gray,
  (Heigho, gray is greet !)
And in a kirtle of green say,
  The green is for maidens meet.

A chaplet on her head she wore,
  (Heigho, the chaplet !)
Of sweet violets therein was store,
  She's sweeter than the violet.

My sheep did leave their wonted food,
  (Heigho, silly sheep !)
And gazed on her as they were wood,
  Wood as he that did them keep.

As the bonny lass passed by,
  (Heigho, bonny lass !)
She roll'd at me with glancing eye,
  As clear as the crystal glass,
All as the sunny beam so bright,
  (Heigho, the sunbeam !)
Glanceth from Phœbus' face forth-right,
  So Love into my heart did stream.

Or as the thunder cleaves the clouds,
  (Heigho, the thunder !)
Wherein the lightsome levin shrouds,
  So cleaves my soul asunder.
Or as dame Cynthia's silver ray,
  (Heigho, the moonlight !)
Upon the glistering wave doth play ;
  Such play is a piteous plight.

The glance into my heart did glide
  (Heigho, the glider !)
Therewith my soul was sharply gride,
  Such wounds some waxen wider.
Hasting to wrench the arrow out,
  (Heigho, Perigot !)
I left the head in my heart-root,
  It was a desperate shot.

There it rankleth aye more and more,
  (Heigho, the arrow !)
Nor can I find salve for my sore,
  Love is a cureless sorrow.

And though my bale with death I bought,
  (Heigho, heavy cheer !)
Yet should this lass not from my thought,
  So you may buy gold too dear.

But whether in painful love I pine,
  (Heigho, pinching pain !)
Or thrive in wealth, she shall be mine,
  But if thou can her obtain.
And if for graceless grief I die,
  (Heigho, graceless grief !)
Witness, she slew me with her eye,
  Let thy folly be the preef.

And you that saw it, simple sheep,
  (Heigho, the fair flock !)
For prief thereof my death shall weep,
  And moan with many a mock.
So learn'd I love on a holy-eve,
  (Heigho, holy-day !)
That ever since my heart did grieve :
  Now endeth our roundelay.
                Finis.   *Edm. Spenser.*

PHYLLIDA AND CORYDON.

IN the merry month of May,
  In a morn by break of day,
Forth I walk'd by the wood-side,
When as May was in his pride :

There I spièd all alone,
Phyllida and Corydon.
Much ado there was, God wot !
He would love and she would not.
She said never man was true ;
He said, none was false to you.
He said, he had loved her long ;
She said, Love should have no wrong.
Corydon would kiss her then ;
She said, maids must kiss no men,
Till they did for good and all ;
Then she made the shepherd call
All the heavens to witness truth
Never loved a truer youth.
Thus with many a pretty oath,
Yea and nay, and faith and troth,
Such as silly shepherds use
When they will not Love abuse,
Love which had been long deluded,
Was with kisses sweet concluded ;
And Phyllida, with garlands gay,
Was made the lady of the May.

   Finis.   *N. Breton.*

TO COLIN CLOUT.

BEAUTY sat bathing in a spring,
 Where fairest shades did hide her ;
The winds blew calm, the birds did sing,
 The cool streams ran beside her.

My wanton thoughts enticed mine eye,
  To see what was forbidden,
But better memory said, fie:
  So, vain desire was chidden.
  Hey nonny, nonny, &c.

Into a slumber then I fell,
  When fond Imagination
Seem'd to see, but could not tell,
  Her feature or her fashion.
But even as babes in dreams do smile,
  And sometimes fall a-weeping,
So I awaked, as wise this while,
  As when I fell a-sleeping.
  Hey nonny, nonny, &c.
          Finis.   *Shepherd Tony.*

ROWLAND'S SONG IN PRAISE OF THE
FAIREST BETA.

O THOU silver Thames, O clearest crystal flood,
  Beta alone the Phœnix is of all thy watery brood;
The queen of virgins only she,
And thou the queen of floods shalt be.
Let all the nymphs be joyful then to see this happy day,
Thy Beta now alone shall be the subject of my lay.

With dainty and delightsome strains of sweetest
    virelays,
Come, lovely shepherds, sit we down and chant our
    Beta's praise.

And let us sing so rare a verse
Our Beta's praises to rehearse,
That little birds shall silent be to hear poor shepherds
    sing,
And rivers backward bend their course, and flow unto
    the spring.

Range all thy swans, fair Thames, together on a rank,
And place them duly one by one upon thy stately bank.
Then set together all a-good,
Recording to the silver flood,
And crave the tuneful nightingale to help ye with her
    lay;
The ousel and the throstle-cock, chief music of our May.

O see what troops of nymphs been sporting on the
    strands;
And they been blessed nymphs of peace, with olives
    in their hands.
How merrily the Muses sing
That all the flowery meadows ring;
And Beta sits upon the bank in purple and in pall,
And she the Queen of Muses is and wears the coronal.

Trim up her golden tresses with Apollo's sacred tree,
O happy sight unto all those that love and honour thee !
The blessed angels have prepared
A glorious crown for thy reward :
Not such a golden crown as haughty Cæsar wears,
But such a glittering starry crown as Ariadne bears.

Make her a goodly chaplet of azured columbine,
And wreath about her coronet with sweetest eglantine.

Bedeck our Beta all with lilies,
And the dainty daffodillies ;
With roses damask, white and red, and fairest fleur-
delice,
With cowslips of Jerusalem, and cloves of paradise.

O thou, fair torch of heaven, the day's most dearest
light,
And thou, bright shining Cynthia, the glory of the
night ;
You stars, the eyes of heaven,
And thou the gliding leven,
And thou, O gorgeous Iris, with all strange colours
dyed ;
When she sheaves forth her rays, then dashed is all
your pride.

See how the day stands still, admiring of her face,
And time, lo ! stretcheth forth his arms, thy Beta to
embrace.
The sirens sing sweet lays,
The Tritons sound her praise,
Go pass on, Thames, and hie thee fast unto the ocean sea,
And let thy billows there proclaim thy Beta's holiday.

And water thou the blessed root of that green olive tree,
With whose sweet shadow all thy banks with peace
preservèd be.
Laurel for poets and conquerors,
And myrtle for Love's-paramours.
That fame may be thy fruit, the boughs preserved by
peace,
And let the mournful cypress die, now storms and
tempests cease.

We'll strew the shore with pearl, where Beta walks
  alone,
And we will pave her princely bower with richest
  Indian stone ;
Perfume the air and make it sweet,
For such a goddess it is meet.
For if her eyes for purity contend with Titan's light,
No marvel then although they so do dazzle human
  sight.

Sound out your trumpets then, from London's stately
  towers,
To beat the stormy winds aback and calm the raging
  showers.
Set to the cornet and the flute,
The orpharion and the lute,
And tune the tabor and the pipe to the sweet violons :
And move the thunder in the air with loudest clarions.

Beta, long may thine altars smoke with yearly sacrifice,
And long thy sacred temples may their sabbaths
  solemnize ;
Thy shepherds watch by day and night,
Thy maids attend the holy light,
And thy large empire stretch her arms from east unto
  the west,   .
And Albion on the Apennines advance her conquering
  crest.

Finis.   *Mich. Drayton.*

THE BARGINET OF ANTIMACHUS.

IN pride of youth, in midst of May,
  When birds with many a merry lay
   Salute the sun's uprising ;
I sat me down fast by a spring,
And while there merry chanters sing,
  I fell upon surmising.
Amidst my doubt and mind's debate,
Of change of time, of world's estate,
  I spied a boy attired
In silver plumes, yet naked quite,
Some pretty feathers fit for flight,
  Wherewith he still aspired.
A bow he bare, to work man's wrack,
A little quiver at his back,
  With many arrows fill'd ;
And in his soft and pretty hand,
He held a lively burning brand,
  Wherewith he lovers kill'd.
Fast by his side, in rich array,
There sat a lovely lady gay,
  His mother as I guess'd,
That set the lad upon her knee,
And trimm'd his bow, and taught him flee,
  And mickle love profess'd.
Oft from her lap at sundry stoures,
He leapt and gather'd summer flowers,
  Both violets and roses :
But see the chance that follow'd fast,
As he the pomp of prime doth waste
  Before that he supposes,

A bee, that harbour'd hard thereby,
Did sting his hand and made him cry,
   Oh, mother, I am wounded !
Fair Venus that beheld her son,
Cried out, Alas ! I am undone :
   And thereupon she swounded.
My little lad, the goddess said,
Who hath my Cupid so dismay'd ?
   He answer'd, Gentle mother,
The honey-worker in the hive
My grief and mischief doth contrive,
   Alas ! it is none other.
She kiss'd the lad : now mark the chance,
And straight she fell into a trance,
   And crying, thus concluded :
Ah ! wanton boy, like to the bee,
Thou with a kiss hast wounded me,
   And hapless Love included.
A little bee doth thee affright,
But ah ! my wounds are full of spright,
   And cannot be recured.
The boy that kiss'd his mother's pain,
Gan smile, and kiss'd her whole again,
   And made her hope assured.
He suck'd the wound, and suaged the sting,
And little Love ycured did sing.
   Then let no lover sorrow :
To-day though grief attaint his heart
Let him with courage bide the smart,
   Amends will come to-morrow.

         Finis.   *Thom. Lodge.*

MENAPHON'S ROUNDELAY.

WHEN tender ewes brought home with evening [1]
             sun
Wend to their folds,
And to their holds
The shepherds trudge when light of day is done :
Upon a tree,
The eagle, Jove's fair bird, did perch,
There resteth he.
A little fly his harbour then did search,
And did presume (though others laugh'd thereat),
To perch whereas the princely eagle sat.

The eagle frown'd and shook his royal wings,
And charged the fly
From thence to hie.
Afraid, in haste the little creature flings,
Yet seeks again,
Fearful, to perk him by the eagle's side.
With moody vein
The speedy post of Ganemede replied :
" Vassal, avaunt, or with my wings you die !
Is't fit an eagle seat him with a fly ?"

The fly craved pity, still the eagle frown'd :
The silly fly,
Ready to die,
Disgraced, displaced, fell grovelling to the ground.
The eagle saw,
And with a royal mind said to the fly :
" Be not in awe,

[1] Ed. 1614 "euening's Sun".

I scorn by me the meanest creature die ;
Then seat thee here : " the joyful fly up-flings,
And sat safe shadow'd with the eagle's wings.

Finis.   *Ro. Greene.*

A PASTORAL OF PHYLLIS AND
CORYDON.

ON a hill there grows a flower,
　　Fair befall the dainty sweet !
By that flower there is a bower,
　　Where the heavenly Muses meet.

In that bower there is a chair,
　　Fringèd all about with gold ;
Where doth sit the fairest fair,
　　That ever eye did yet behold.

It is Phyllis fair and bright,
　　She that is the shepherds' joy ;
She that Venus did despite,
　　And did blind her little boy.

This is she, the wise, the rich,
　　That the world desires to see ;
This is *ipsa quæ* the which
　　There is none but only she.

Who would not this face admire ?
　　Who would not this saint adore ?

E

Who would not this sight desire,
  Though he thought to see no more?

Oh, fair eyes! yet let me see
  One good look, and I am gone;
Look on me, for I am he,
  Thy poor silly Corydon.

Thou that art the shepherds' queen,
  Look upon thy silly swain;
By thy comfort have been seen
  Dead men brought to life again.

            Finis.   *N. Breton.*

CORYDON AND MELAMPUS' SONG.

Cor.

MELAMPUS, when will Love be void of fears?
    Mel. When Jealousy hath neither eyes nor
      ears.
Cor. Melampus, when will Love be throughly
      shrieved?
Mel. When it is hard to speak, and not believed.
Cor. Melampus, when is Love most malcontent?
Mel. When lovers range, and bear their bows unbent.
Cor. Melampus, tell me, when Love takes least harm?
Mel. When swains' sweet pipes are puff'd, and trulls
      are warm.
Cor. Melampus, tell me, when is Love best fed?
Mel. When it has suck'd the sweet that ease hath bred.

Cor. Melampus, when is time in love ill-spent ?
Mel. When it earns meed and yet receives no rent.
Cor. Melampus, when is time well spent in love ?
Mel. When deeds win meed, and words love's works
      do prove.

          Finis.   *Geor. Pœle.*

TITYRUS TO HIS FAIR PHYLLIS.

THE silly swain whose love breeds discontent,
  Thinks death a trifle, life a loathsome thing,
    Sad he looks, sad he lies ;
But when his fortune's malice doth relent,
Then of Love's sweetness he will sweetly sing ;
    Thus he lives, thus he dies.
Then Tityrus whom Love hath happy made,
Will rest thrice happy in this myrtle shade ;
    For though Love at first did grieve him,
    Yet did Love at last relieve him.

          Finis.   *I. D.*

[LOVE'S THRALL.]

Shepherd.

SWEET thrall, first step to Love's felicity !
  Shepherdess. Sweet thrall, no stop to perfect
  liberty !

He. O life ! *She.* What life?
He. Sweet life.   *She.* No life more sweet :
He. O Love ! *She.* What Love?
He. Sweet Love.   *She.* No Love more meet.

Finis.   *I. M.*

ANOTHER BY THE SAME AUTHOR.

FIELDS were overspread with flowers,
　Fairest choice of Flora's treasure ;
Shepherds there had shady bowers,
Where they oft reposed with pleasure :
　　Meadows flourish'd fresh and gay,
　　Where the wanton herds did play.

Springs more clear than crystal streams
Seated were the groves among,
Thus nor Titan's scorching beams,
Nor earth's drouth could shepherds wrong :
　　Fair Pomona's fruitful pride
　　Did the budding branches hide.

Flocks of sheep fed on the plains,
Harmless sheep that roam'd at large ;
Here and there sat pensive swains,
Waiting on their wandering charge :
　　Pensive while their lasses smiled,
　　Lasses which had them beguiled.

Hills with trees were richly dight,
Valleys stored with Vesta's wealth ;

Both did harbour sweet delight,
Nought was there to hinder health :
    Thus did heaven grace the soil,
    Not deform'd with workmen's toil.

Purest plot of earthly mould,
Might that land be justly named ;
Art by nature was controll'd,
Art, which no such pleasures framed.
    Fairer place was never seen ;
    Fittest place for beauty's queen.
       Finis.   *I. M.*

MENAPHON TO PERSANA.

FAIR fields, proud Flora's vaunt, why is't you smile
    Whenas I languish ?
You golden meads, why shine you to beguile
    My weeping anguish ?
I live to sorrow, you to pleasure spring,
    Why do ye spring thus ?
What, will not Boreas, tempests' wrathful king,
    Take some pity on us ?
And send forth Winter in her rusty weed,
    To wail my bemoanings,
While I distress'd do tune my country reed
    Unto my groanings ?
But heaven and earth, time, place, and every power
    Have with her conspired

To turn my blissful sweet to baleful sour,
    Since I this desired.
The heaven whereto my thoughts may not aspire,
    Aye me unhappy !
It was my fault t' embrace my bane the fire
    That forceth me die.
Mine be the pain, but her's the cruel cause
    Of this strange torment :
Wherefore no time my banning prayers shall pause
    Till proud she repent.
     Finis.   *Ro. Greene.*

A SWEET PASTORAL.

GOOD Muse, rock me asleep
  With some sweet harmony ;
The weary eye is not to keep
  Thy wary company.

Sweet Love, begone awhile,
  Thou knowest my heaviness ;
Beauty is born but to beguile
  My heart of happiness.

See how my little flock,
  That loved to feed on high,
Do headlong tumble down the rock,
  And in the valley die.

The bushes and the trees
　That were so fresh and green,
Do all their dainty colour leese,
　And not a leaf is seen.

The blackbird and the thrush
　That made the woods to ring,
With all the rest are now at hush,
　And not a note they sing.

Sweet Philomel, the bird
　That hath the heavenly throat,
Doth now, alas ! not once afford
　Recording of a note.

The flowers have had a frost,
　Each herb hath lost her savour,
And Phyllida the fair hath lost
　The comfort of her favour.

Now all these careful sights
　So kill me in conceit,
That how to hope upon delights,
　It is but mere deceit.

And therefore, my sweet Muse,
　Thou knowest what help is best ;
Do now thy heavenly cunning use,
　To set my heart at rest.

And in a dream bewray
　What fate shall be my friend,
Whether my life shall still decay,
　Or when my sorrow end.
　　　　　　Finis.　　　　　*N. Breton.*

HARPALUS' COMPLAINT ON PHYLLIDA'S
LOVE BESTOWED ON CORIN,

WHO LOVED HER NOT, AND DENIED HIM THAT
LOVED HER.

PHYLLIDA was a fair maid,
   As fresh as any flower,
Whom Harpalus the herdsman pray'd
   To be his paramour.
Harpalus and eke Corin
   Were herdsmen both yfere ;
And Phyllida could twist and spin,
   And thereto sing full clear.
But Phyllida was all too coy,
   For Harpalus to win ;
For Corin was her only joy,
   Who forced her not a pin.
How often would she flowers twine,
   How often garlands make
Of cowslips and of columbine,
   And all for Corin's sake?
But Corin he had hawks to lure,
   And forcèd more the field ;
Of lover's law he took no cure,
   For once he was beguiled.
Harpalus prevailèd nought,
   His labour all was lost ;
For he was furthest from her thought,
   And yet he loved her most.

Therefore wox he both pale and lean,
  And dry as clod of clay;
His flesh it was consumèd clean,
  His colour gone away.
His beard it had not long been shave,
  His hair hung all unkempt;
A man most fit even for the grave,
  Whom spiteful love had spent.
His eyes were red, and all forewatch'd,
  His face besprent with tears;
It seem'd unhap had him long hatch'd,
  In midst of his despairs.
His clothes were black and also bare,
  As one forlorn was he;
Upon his head he always ware
  A wreath of willow-tree.
His beasts he kept upon the hill,
  And he sat in the dale;
And thus with sighs and sorrows shrill,
  He gan to tell his tale.
O Harpalus! thus would he say,
  Unhappiest under sun,
The cause of thine unhappy day,
  By love was first begun.
For thou went'st first by suit to seek
  A tiger to make tame,
That sets not by thy love a leek,
  But makes thy grief a game.
As easy were it to convert
  The frost into a flame,
As for to turn a froward heart
  Whom thou so fain wouldst frame,
Corin, he liveth careless,

He leaps among the leaves,
He eats the fruit of thy redress;
　Thou reap'st, he takes the sheaves.
My beasts, awhile your food refrain,
　And hark your herdman's sound,
Whom spiteful Love, alas! hath slain,
　Through-girt with many a wound.
Oh! happy be ye beasts wild,
　That here your pasture takes;
I see that ye be not beguiled,
　Of these your faithful makes.
The hart he feedeth by the hind,
　The buck hard by the doe,
The turtle-dove is not unkind
　To him that loves her so.
The ewe she hath by her the ram,
　The young cow hath the bull;
The calf with many a lusty lamb
　Do feed their hunger full.
But, well-away! that Nature wrought
　Thee, Phyllida, so fair;
For I may say that I have bought
　Thy beauty all too dear.
What reason is't that cruelty
　With beauty should have part?
Or else that such great tyranny,
　Should dwell in woman's heart?
I see therefore to shape my death,
　She cruelly is prest;
To th' end that I may want my breath,
　My days been at the best.
O Cupid! grant this my request,
　And do not stop thine ears:

That she may feel within her breast
　The pain of my despairs.
Of Corin that is careless,
　That she may crave her fee ;
As I have done, in great distress,
　That loved her faithfully.
But since that I shall die her slave,
　Her slave and eke her thrall,
Write you, my friends, upon my grave,
　This chance that is befall :
Here lieth unhappy Harpalus,
　By cruel love now slain,
Whom Phyllida unjustly thus,
　Hath murder'd with disdain.
　　　Finis.　L. T. Howard, Earl of Surrey.

ANOTHER ON THE SAME SUBJECT, BUT MADE AS IT WERE IN ANSWER.

ON a goodly summer's day,
　Harpalus and Phyllida,
He a true-hearted swain,
She full of coy disdain,
　Drove their flocks to field ;
He to see his shepherdess,
She did dream on nothing less
Than his continual care,
Which to grim-faced Despair
　Wholly did him yield.
Corin she affected still,
All the more thy heart to kill ;

Thy case doth make me rue
That thou shouldst love so true,
    And be thus disdain'd !
While their flocks a-feeding were,
They did meet together there ;
Then with a curtsy low,
And sighs that told his woe,
    Thus to her he plain'd :
" Bide awhile, fair Phyllida,
List what Harpalus will say
Only in love to thee ;
Though thou respect not me,
    Yet vouchsafe an ear
To prevent ensuing ill,
Which no doubt betide thee will ;
If thou do not foresee
To shun it presently,
    Then thy harm I fear.
Firm thy love is, well I wot,
To the man that loves thee not ;
Lovely and gentle maid,
Thy hope is quite betray'd,
    Which my heart doth grieve.
Corin is unkind to thee,
Though thou think contrary ;
His love is grown as light,
As is his falcon's flight ;
    This, sweet nymph, believe.
Mopsus' daughter, that young maid,
Her bright eyes his heart hath stray'd
From his affecting thee ;
[K]now there is none but she
    That is Corin's bliss.

Phyllis men the virgin call ;
She is buxom, fair, and tall,
Yet not like Phyllida,—
If I my mind might say,
      Eyes oft deem amiss.
He commends her beauty rare,
Which with thine may not compare ;
He does extol her eye,
Silly thing, if thine were by :
      Thus conceit can err.
He is ravish'd with her breath,
Thine can quicken life in death ;
He praiseth all her parts,
Thine wins a world of hearts,
      More if more there were.
Look, sweet nymph, upon thy flock,
They stand still, and now feed not,
As if they shared with thee
Grief for this injury
      Offer'd to true love.
Pretty lambkins, how they moan,
And in bleating seem to groan,
That any shepherd swain
Should cause their mistress pain
      By affects' remove.
If you look but on the grass,
It's not half so green as 'twas
When I began my tale,
But it is wither'd pale,
      All in mere remorse.
Mark the trees that bragg'd even now
Of each goodly green-leaved bough,
They seem as blasted all,

Ready for winter's fall :
    Such is true love's force.
The gentle murmur of the springs
Are become contrary things ;
They have forgot their pride,
And quite forsake their glide,
    As if charm'd they stand.
And the flowers growing by,
Late so fresh in every eye ;
See how they hang the head,
As on a sudden dead,
    Dropping on the sand.
The birds that chanted it erewhile,
Ere they heard of Corin's guile,
Sit as they were afraid,
Or by some hap dismay'd,
    For this wrong to thee.
Hark, sweet Phil, how Philomel,
That was wont to sing so well,
Jargles now in yonder bush,
Worser than the rudest thrush,
    As it were not she."
Phyllida, who all this while
Neither gave a sigh or smile,
Round about the field did gaze,
As her wits were in a maze,
    Poor despisèd maid ;
And revivèd at the last,
After streams of tears were past,
Leaning on her shepherd's hook,
With a sad and heavy look,
    The poor soul she said :
"Harpalus, I thank not thee,

For this sorry tale to me ;
Meet me here again to-morrow,
Then I will conclude my sorrow,
    Mildly, if may be."
With their flocks they home do fare,
Either's heart too full of care ;
If they do meet again,
Then what they further sayn
    You shall hear from me.
                    Finis.   *Shep. Tony.*

THE NYMPHS MEETING THEIR MAY
QUEEN, ENTERTAIN HER WITH
THIS DITTY.

WITH fragrant flowers we strew the way,
    And make this our chief holiday ;
For though this clime were blest of yore,
Yet was it never proud before :
    O beauteous queen of second Troy,
    Accept of our unfeignèd joy.

Now th' air is sweeter than sweet balm
And satyrs dance about the palm ;
Now earth with verdure newly dight,
Gives perfect signs of her delight.
    O beauteous queen, &c.

Now birds record new harmony,'
And trees do whistle melody;
Now everything that Nature breeds,
Doth clad itself in pleasant weeds.
     O beauteous queen, &c.
          Finis.   *Tho. Watson.*

COLIN CLOUT'S MOURNFUL DITTY FOR

THE DEATH OF ASTROPHEL.

SHEPHERDS that wont on pipes of oaten reed
     Ofttimes to plain your love's concealèd smart,
And with your piteous lays have learnt to breed
Compassion in a country lass's heart :
Hearken, ye gentle shepherds, to my song,
And place my doleful plaint your plaints among,

To you alone I sing this mournful verse,
The mournfull'st verse that ever man heard tell ;
To you whose soften'd hearts it may impierce
With dolour's dart for death of Astrophel :
To you I sing, and to none other wight,
For, well I wot, my rhymes been rudely dight.

Yet as they been, if any nicer wit
Shall hap to hear or covet them to read,
Think he that such are for such ones most fit,
Made not to please the living but the dead :
And if in him found pity ever place,
Let him be moved to pity such a case.
          Finis.   *Edm. Spenser.*

DAMÆTAS' JIG IN PRAISE OF HIS LOVE.

JOLLY shepherd, shepherd on a hill,
  On a hill so merrily,
  On a hill so cheerily,
Fear not, shepherd, there to pipe thy fill,
Fill every dale, fill every plain :
  Both sing and say, " Love feels no pain."

Jolly shepherd, shepherd on a green,
  On a green so merrily,
  On a green so cheerily,
Be thy voice shrill, be thy mirth seen,
Heard to each swain, seen to each trull :
  Both sing and say, " Love's joy is full."

Jolly shepherd, shepherd in the sun,
  In the sun so merrily,
  In the sun so cheerily,
Sing forth thy songs, and let thy rhymes run
Down to the dales from [1] the hills above :
  Both sing and say, " No life to love."

Jolly shepherd, shepherd in the shade,
  In the shade so merrily,
  In the shade so cheerily,
Joy in thy life, life of shepherd's trade,
Joy in thy love, love full of glee :
  Both sing and say, " Sweet Love for me."

[1] Old eds. " to."

F

Jolly shepherd, shepherd here or there,
   Here or there so merrily,
   Here or there so cheerily,
Or in thy chat, either at thy cheer,
In every jig, in every lay
   Both sing and say, "Love lasts for aye."

Jolly shepherd, shepherd Daphnis' love,
   Daphnis' love so merrily,
   Daphnis' love so cheerily,
Let thy fancy never more remove,
Fancy be fix'd, fix'd not to fleet :
   Still sing and say, "Love's yoke is sweet."
         Finis.   *John Wootton.*

MONTANUS' PRAISE OF HIS FAIR PHŒBE.

PHŒBE sat,
   Sweet she sat,
  Sweet sat Phœbe when I saw her,
White her brow,
Coy her eye,
  Brow and eye, how much you please me !
Words I spent,
Sighs I sent,
  Sighs and words could never draw her.
Oh, my love !
Thou art lost,
  Since no sight could ever ease thee.
Phœbe sat
By a fount,
  Sitting by a fount I spied her,

Sweet her touch,
Rare her voice,
  Touch and voice what may distain you !
As she sung,
I did sigh,
  And by sighs whilst that I tried her,
Oh, mine eyes !
You did lose
  Her first sight, whose want did pain you.
Phœbe's flocks
White as wool,
  Yet were Phœbe's looks more whiter,
Phœbe's eyes
Dovelike mild,
  Dovelike eyes both mild and cruel ;
Montane swears
In your lamps
  He will die for to delight her.
Phœbe yield,
Or I die ;
  Shall true hearts be fancy's fuel?

                Finis.   *Thom. Lodge.*

THE COMPLAINT OF THESTILIS THE
FORSAKEN SHEPHERD.

THESTILIS, a silly swain, when love did him
    forsake,
In mournful wise amid the woods thus 'gan his plaint
    to make.

Ah! woful man, quoth he, fall'n is thy lot to moan,
And pine away with careful thoughts unto thy love
    unknown.
Thy nymph forsakes thee quite, whom thou didst
    honour so,
That aye to her thou wert a friend, but to thyself
    a foe.
Ye lovers that have lost your heart's desirèd choice,
Lament with me my cruel hap and help my trembling
    voice.
Was never man that stood so great in fortune's grace,
Nor with his sweet (alas! too dear) possess'd so high
    a place,
As I whose simple heart aye thought himself still
    sure,
But now I see high-springing tides they may not aye
    endure.
She knows my guiltless heart, and yet she lets it
    pine ;
Of her untrue professèd love so feeble is the twine.
What wonder is it then if I berent my hairs,
And craving death continually, do bathe myself in
    tears?
When Crœsus, King of Lyde, was cast in cruel bands,
And yielded goods and life into his enemy's hands,
What tongue could tell his woe? yet was his grief
    much less
Than mine, for I have lost my love which might my
    woe redress.
Ye woods that shroud my limbs, give now your hollow
    sound
That ye may help me to bewail the cares that me
    confound.

Ye rivers, rest awhile, and stay your streams that run ;
Rue Thestilis, the wofull'st man that rests under the
    sun.
Transport my sighs, ye winds, unto my pleasant foe ;
My trickling tears shall witness bear of this my cruel
    woe.
Oh ! happy man were I if all the gods agreed
That now the sisters three should cut in twain my
    fatal thread !
Till life with love shall end, I here resign all joy,
Thy pleasant sweet I now lament whose lack breeds
    mine annoy.
Farewell, my dear, therefore, farewell to me well
    known ;
If that I die, it shall be said that thou hast slain
    thine own.

            Finis.   *L. T. Howard. E. of Surrey.*

TO PHYLLIS THE FAIR SHEPHERDESS.

MY Phyllis hath the morning sun,
    At first to look upon her ;
And Phyllis hath morn-waking birds,
    Her risings still to honour.
My Phyllis hath prime-feather'd flowers,
    That smile when she treads on them ;
And Phyllis hath a gallant flock,
    That leaps since she doth own them.
But Phyllis hath too hard a heart,
    Alas, that she should have it !

It yields no mercy to desert,
Nor grace to those that crave it.
Sweet sun, when thou look'st on,
Pray her regard my moan;
Sweet birds, when you sing to her,
To yield some pity, woo her;
Sweet flowers, that she treads on,
Tell her, her beauty deads one.
And if in life her love she nill agree me,
Pray her before I die she will come see me.

Finis.   S. E. D.

THE SHEPHERD DORON'S JIG.

THROUGH the shrubs as I can crack,
        For my lambs, pretty ones,
        'Mongst many little ones,
Nymphs I mean, whose hair was black
            As the crow,
            Like as the snow
Her face and brow shined I ween,
        I saw a little one,
        A bonny pretty one,
As bright, buxom, and as sheen
                As was she
                On her knee
That lull'd the god whose arrows warms
        Such merry little ones,
        Such fair-faced pretty ones,

As dally in Love's chiefest harms.
Such was mine
Whose grey eyen
Made me love ; I gan to woo
This sweet little one,
This bonny pretty one.
I woo'd hard a day or two,
Till she bade,
"Be not sad,
Woo no more, I am thine own,
Thy dearest little one,
Thy truest pretty one."
Thus was faith and firm love shown,
As behoves
Shepherds' loves.

Finis.   *Ro. Greene.*

ASTROPHEL'S SONG OF PHYLLIDA AND CORYDON.

FAIR in a morn, (O fairest morn !)
    Was never morn so fair,
There shone a sun, though not the sun
    That shineth in the air.
For[1] the earth, and from the earth,
    (Was never such a creature !)

---

[1] A MS. copy (see Grosart's edition of Breton's Works)
reads :—
"For of the earth and from the earth, though not an earthly
    creature," &c.

Did come this face (was never face
  That carried such a feature).
Upon a hill, (O blessed hill !
  Was never hill so blessed,)
There stood a man (was never man
  For woman so distressed) :
This man beheld a heavenly view,
  Which did such virtue give
As clears the blind, and helps[1] the lame,
  And makes the dead man live.
This man had hap, (O happy man !
  More happy none than he ;)
For he had hap to see the hap
  That none had hap to see.
This silly swain, (and silly swains
  Are men of meanest grace :)
Had yet the grace, (O gracious gift ![2])
  To hap on such a face.
He pity cried, and pity came,
  And pitied so his pain,
As dying would not let him die,
  But gave him life again.
For joy whereof he made such mirth
  As all the woods did ring ;
And Pan with all his swains came forth
  To hear the shepherd sing ;
But such a song sung never was,
  Nor shall be sung again,
Of Phyllida the shepherds' queen,
  And Corydon the swain.
Fair Phyllis is the shepherds' queen,
  (Was never such a queen as she,)

---

[1] MS. "heals."   [2] So MS.—*England's Helicon* "guest."

And Corydon her only swain
   (Was never such a swain as he):
Fair[1] Phyllis hath the fairest face
   That ever eye did yet behold,
And Corydon the constant'st faith
   That ever yet kept flock in fold ;
Sweet Phyllis is the sweetest sweet
   That ever yet the earth did yield,
And Corydon the kindest swain
   That ever yet kept[2] lambs in field.
Sweet Philomel is Phyllis' bird,
   Though Corydon be he that caught her,
And Corydon doth hear her sing,
   Though Phyllida be she that taught her :
Poor Corydon doth keep the fields,
   Though Phyllida be she that owes them,
And Phyllida doth walk the meads,
   Though Corydon be he that mows them :
The little lambs are Phyllis' love,
   Though Corydon is he that feeds them,
The gardens fair are Phyllis' ground,
   Though Corydon is he that weeds them.
Since then that Phyllis only is
   The only shepherd's only queen ;
And Corydon the only swain
   That only hath her shepherd been,—

---

[1] The MS. reads :—
" Faire Phillis hath the fairest witt that euer yett the world did
    breede,
And Coridon the truest hart that euer yett ware shepherdes
    weede.
Sweete Phillis is the onlie sweete," &c.
[2] MS. " did keep the fielde."

Though Phyllis keep her bower of state,
Shall Corydon consume away?
No, shepherd, no, work out the week,
And Sunday shall be holiday.

Finis.   *N. Breton.*

THE PASSIONATE SHEPHERD'S SONG.

ON a day, (alack the day!)
Love whose month was ever May,
Spied a blossom passing fair,
Playing in the wanton air.
Through the velvet leaves the wind
All unseen gan passage find,
That the shepherd (sick to death)
Wish'd himself the heaven's breath.
Air, quoth he, thy cheeks may blow;
Air, would I might triumph so.
But, alas! my hand hath sworn,
Ne'er to pluck thee from thy thorn.
Vow, alack! for youth unmeet,
Youth so apt to pluck a sweet;
Thou for whom Jove would swear
Juno but an Ethiope were,
And deny himself for Jove,
Turning mortal for thy[1] love.

Finis.   *W. Shakespeare.*

[1] Old eds. "my."

THE UNKNOWN SHEPHERD'S
COMPLAINT.

M Y flocks feed not, my ewes breed not,
　　My rams speed not, all is amiss :
Love is denying, Faith is defying ;
Heart's renying, causer of this.
All my merry jigs are quite forgot,
All my lady's love is lost, God wot ;
Where her faith was firmly fix'd in love,
There a nay is placed without remove.
　　　　One silly cross wrought all my loss ;
　　　　O frowning fortune, cursed fickle dame !
　　　　For now I see inconstancy
　　　　More in women than in men remain.

In black mourn I, all fears scorn I,
Love hath forlorn me, living in thrall ;
Heart is bleeding, all help needing,
O cruel speeding, fraughted with gall.
My shepherd's pipe can sound no deal,
My wether's bell rings doleful knell.
My curtail dog that wont to have play'd,
Plays not at all, but seems afraid ;
　　　　With sighs so deep, procures to weep,
　　　　In howling-wise to see my doleful plight.
　　　　How sighs resound, through heartless ground,
　　　　Like a thousand vanquish'd men in bloody fight !

Clear wells spring not, sweet birds sing not,
Green plants bring not forth their dye ;
Herds stand weeping, flocks all sleeping,
Nymphs back peeping fearfully.
All our pleasure known to us poor swains,
All our merry meeting on the plains,
All our evening sports from us are fled,
All our love is lost, for Love is dead.
    Farewell, sweet Love, thy like ne'er was,
    For sweet content, the cause of all my moan :
    Poor Corydon must live alone ;
    Other help for him, I see that there is none.
        Finis.   *Ignoto.*

ANOTHER OF THE SAME SHEPHERD'S.

AS it fell upon a day,
In the merry month of May,
Sitting in a pleasant shade,
Which a group of myrtles made,
Beasts did leap and birds did sing,
Trees did grow and plants did spring,
Everything did banish moan,
Save the nightingale alone ;
She, poor bird, as all forlorn,
Lean'd her breast against a thorn,
And there sung the dolefull'st ditty,
That to hear it was great pity.
Fie, fie, fie! now would she cry ;
Teru, teru, by-and-by.

That to hear her so complain
Scarce I could from tears refrain,
For her griefs so lively shown
Made me think upon mine own.
Ah, thought I, thou mourn'st in vain,
None takes pity on thy pain.
Senseless trees, they cannot hear thee ;
Ruthless beasts,[1] they will not cheer thee ;
King Pandion he is dead,
All thy friends are lapp'd in lead ;
All thy fellow birds do sing,
Careless of thy sorrowing ;
Even so, poor bird, like thee,
None alive will pity me.

Finis.   *Ignoto.*

THE SHEPHERD'S ALLUSION OF HIS OWN AMOROUS INFELICITY TO THE OFFENCE OF ACTÆON.

ACTÆON lost in middle of his sport
Both shape and life for looking but awry ;
Diana was afraid he would report
What secrets he had seen in passing by.
     To tell but truth, the self-same hurt have I,
     By viewing her for whom I daily die.
I leese my wonted shape, in that my mind

---

[1] In *The Passionate Pilgrim,* 1599, the reading is " Ruthless Beares."

Doth suffer wreck upon the stony rock
Of her disdain, who contrary to kind
Does bear a breast more hard than any stock ;
 And former form of limbs is changèd quite
 By cares in love, and want of due delight.
I leese my life, in that each secret thought
Which I conceive through wanton fond regard,
Doth make me say that life availeth nought
Where service cannot have a due reward.
 I dare not name the nymph that works my smart,
 Though Love hath grav'n her name within my heart.
    Finis.   *T. Watson.*

MONTANUS' SONNET TO HIS FAIR
PHŒBE.

A TURTLE sat upon a leafless tree,
 Mourning her absent phere,
 With sad and sorry cheer ;
 About her wondering stood,
 The citizens of wood,
 And whilst her plumes she rents,
 And for her love laments,
 The stately trees complain them,
 The birds with sorrow pain them ;
 Each one that doth her view,
 Her pains and sorrows rue :
 But where the sorrows known,
 That me hath overthrown,
Oh, how would Phœbe sigh if she did look on me !

The lovesick Polypheme that could not see,
  Who on the barren shore
  His fortunes did deplore,
  And melteth all in moan
  For Galatea gone,
  And with his piteous[1] cries
  Afflicts both earth and skies,
  And to his woe betook
  Doth break both pipe and hook ;
  For whom complains the morn,
  For whom the sea-nymphs mourn :
  Alas ! his pain is nought,
  For were my woe but thought,
Oh, how would Phœbe sigh if she did look on me !

  Beyond compare my pain,
    Yet glad am I,
  If gentle Phœbe deign
    To see her Montane die.
              Finis.   *Thom. Lodge.*

PHŒBE'S SONNET, A REPLY TO
MONTANUS' PASSION.

" DOWN a down !"
      Thus Phyllis sung,
      By fancy once distress'd :

[1] The word "piteous" is omitted in *England's Helicon,* but found in Lodge's *Rosalind,* 1590.

" Whoso by foolish Love are stung
  Are worthily oppress'd.
And so sing I, with down a down."

" When Love was first begot,
And by the mother's will,
Did fall to human lot,
His solace to fulfil,
Devoid of all deceit,
A chaste and holy fire,
Did quicken men's conceit,
And women's breasts inspire.
The gods that saw the good,
That mortals did approve,
With kind and holy mood
Began to talk of Love.
  Down a down !"
    Thus Phyllis sung
    By fancy once distress'd, &c.

" But during this accord,
A wonder strange to hear,
Whilst Love in deed and word,
Most faithful did appear,
False Semblance came in place,
By Jealousy attended,
And with a double face
Both love and fancy blended ;
Which made the gods forsake,
And men from fancy fly,
And maidens scorn a make ;
Forsooth, and so will I.

Down a down !"
  Thus Phyllis sung,
  By fancy once distress'd:
" Whoso by foolish Love are stung,
  . Are worthily oppress'd.
And so sing I, with down a down."

Finis.   *Thom. Lodge.*

CORYDON'S SUPPLICATION TO PHYLLIS.

S WEET Phyllis, if a silly swain
        May sue to thee for grace,
See not thy loving shepherd slain
  With looking on thy face ;
But think what power thou hast got,
  Upon my flock and me;
Thou seest they now regard me not,
  But all do follow thee.
And if I have so far presumed,
  With prying in thine eyes,
Yet let not comfort be consumed
  That in thy pity lies ;
But as thou art that Phyllis fair,
  That fortune favour gives,
So let not love die in despair
  That in thy favour lives.
The deer do browse upon the briar,
  The birds do pick the cherries ;
And will not Beauty grant Desire
  One handful of her berries ?

G

If it be so that thou hast sworn
   That none shall look on thee,
Yet let me know thou dost not scorn
   To cast a look on me.
But if thy beauty make thee proud,
   Think then what is ordain'd ;
The heavens have never yet allow'd
   That love should be disdain'd.
Then lest the fates that favour love
   Should curse thee for unkind,
Let me report for thy behoof,
   The honour of thy mind ;
Let Corydon with full consent
   Set down what he hath seen,
That Phyllida with Love's content
   Is sworn the shepherds' queen.
           Finis.   *N. Breton.*

DAMÆTAS' MADRIGAL IN PRAISE OF HIS DAPHNIS.

TUNE on my pipe the praises of my love,
   Love fair and bright ;
Fill earth with sound, and airy heavens above,
   Heavens Jove's delight,
   With Daphnis' praise.

To pleasant Tempe groves and plains about,
   Plains shepherds' pride ;

Resounding echoes of her praise ring out,
    Ring far and wide
    My Daphnis' praise.

When I begin to sing, begin to sound,
    Sounds loud and shrill ;
Do make each note unto the skies rebound,
    Skies calm and still,
      With Daphnis' praise.

Her tresses are like wires of beaten gold,
    Gold bright and sheen ;
Like Nisus' golden hair that Scylla poll'd,
    Scyll o'erseen
    Through Minos' love.

Her eyes like shining lamps in midst of night,
    Night dark and dead,
Or as the stars that give the seamen light,
    Light for to lead
    Their wand'ring ships.

Amidst her cheeks the rose and lily strive,
    Lily snow-white,
When their contend doth make their colour thrive,
    Colour too bright
    For shepherds' eyes.

Her lips like scarlet of the finest dye,
    Scarlet blood-red ;
Teeth white as snow which on the hills doth lie,
    Hills overspread
    By Winter's force.

Her skin as soft as is the finest silk,
  Silk soft and fine,
Of colour like unto the whitest milk,
  Milk of the kine
  Of Daphnis' herd.

As swift of foot as is the pretty roe,
  Roe swift of pace,
When yelping hounds pursue her to and fro,
  Hounds fierce in chase,
  To reave her life.

Cease tongues to tell of any more compares,
  Compares too rude,
Daphnis' deserts and beauty are too rare :
  Then here conclude
  Fair Daphnis' praise.
            Finis.   *J. Wootton.*

DORON'S DESCRIPTION OF HIS FAIR
SHEPHERDESS SAMELA.

LIKE to Diana in her summer weed,
  Girt with a crimson robe of brightest dye,
    Goes fair Samela.
Whiter than be the flocks that straggling feed,
When wash'd by Arethusa faint they lie,
    Is fair Samela.
As fair Aurora in her morning gray,
Deck'd with the ruddy glister of her love,
    Is fair Samela.

Like lovely Thetis on a calmèd day,
Whenas her brightness Neptune's fancies move,
      Shines fair Samela.
Her tresses gold, her eyes like glassy streams,
Her teeth are pearl, the breasts are ivory,
      Of fair Samela.
Her cheeks like rose and lily yield forth gleams,
Her brows' bright arches framed of ebony ;
      Thus fair Samela
Passeth fair Venus in her brightest hue,
And Juno, in the show of majesty :
      For she's Samela.
Pallas in wit, all three if you well view,
For beauty, wit, and matchless dignity,
      Yield to Samela.
          Finis.   *Ro. Greene.*

WODENFRIDE'S SONG IN PRAISE OF

AMARGANA.

THE sun, the season, in each thing
   Revives new pleasures, the sweet spring
Hath put to flight the winter keen,
To glad our lovely summer queen.

The paths where Amargana treads
With flow'ry tap'stries Flora spreads,
And Nature clothes the ground in green,
To glad our lovely summer queen.

The groves put on their rich array,
With hawthorn blooms embroider'd gay ;
And sweet perfumed with eglantine,
To glad our lovely summer queen.

The silent river stays his course,
Whilst playing on the crystal source ;
The silver scalèd fish are seen
To glad our lovely summer queen.

The woods at her fair sight rejoices
The little birds with their loud voices
In concert on the briars been,
To glad our lovely summer queen.

The fleecy flocks do scud and skip,
The wood-nymphs, fauns, and satyrs trip
And dance the myrtle trees between,
To glad our lovely summer queen.

Great Pan, our god, for her dear sake,
This feast and meeting bids us make,
Of shepherds, lads, and lasses sheen,
To glad our lovely summer queen.

And every swain his chance doth prove,
To win fair Amargana's love ;
In sporting strife, quite void of spleen,
To glad our lovely summer queen.

All happiness let heaven her lend,
And all the Graces her attend ;
Thus bid me pray the Muses Nine,
Long live our lovely summer queen.

Finis.　　　　　　　　*W. H.*

ANOTHER OF THE SAME.

H APPY shepherds, sit and see,
　　　With joy,
　　The peerless wight
For whose sake Pan keeps from ye
　　　Annoy,
　　And gives delight,
Blessing this pleasant spring.
Her praises must I sing :
List, you swains, list to me,
The whiles your flocks feeding be.

First, her brow a beauteous globe
　　　I deem,
　　And golden hair ;
And her cheek Aurora's robe
　　　Doth seem,
　　But far more fair.
Her eyes like stars are bright,
And dazzle with their light ;
Rubies her lips to see,
But to taste nectar they be.

Orient pearls her teeth, her smile
　　　Doth link
　　The Graces three ;
Her white neck doth eyes beguile
　　　To think
　　It ivory.

Alas! her lily hand
How it doth me command!
Softer silk none can be,
And whiter milk none can see.

Circe's wand is not so straight
    As is
      Her body small;
But two pillars bear the weight
    Of this
      Majestic hall.
Those be, I you assure,
Of alablaster pure;
Polish'd fine in each part:
Ne'er Nature yet show'd like art.

How shall I her pretty tread
    Express
      When she doth walk?
Scarce she does the primrose head
    Depress,
      Or tender stalk
Of blue-vein'd violets,
Whereon her foot she sets.
Virtuous she is, for we find
In body fair beauteous [1] mind.

Live fair Amargana still
    Extoll'd
      In all my rhyme;
Hand want art, when I want will
    T'unfold
      Her worth divine.

    [1] Ed. 1614, " a beaut'ous."

But now my muse doth rest,
Despair closed in my breast.
Of the valour I sing;
Weake faith that no hope doth bring.

Finis.   *W. H.*

AN EXCELLENT PASTORAL DITTY.

A CAREFUL nymph, with careless grief opprest,
  Under the shadow of an ashen tree,
With lute in hand did paint out her unrest,
  Unto a nymph that bare her company;
    No sooner had she tunèd every string,
    But sobb'd and sigh'd, and thus began to sing :—

Ladies, and nymphs, come listen to my plaint,
  On whom the cheerful sun did never rise ;
If pity's strokes your tender breasts may taint,
  Come learn of me to wet your wanton eyes,
    For Love in vain the name of pleasure bears ;
    His sweet delights are turnèd into fears.

The trustless shows, the frights, the feeble joys,
  The freezing doubts, the guileful promises,
The feignèd looks, the shifts, the subtle toys,
  The brittle hope, the stedfast heaviness,
    The wishèd war in such uncertain peace ;
    These with my woe, my woes with these increase.

Thou dreadful god, that in thy mother's lap
  Dost lie, and hear the cry of my complaint,
And seest, and smilest at my sore mishap,
  That lack but skill my sorrows here to paint;
    Thy fire from heaven before the hurt I spied,
    Quite through mine eyes into my breast did glide.

My life was light, my blood did spirt and spring,
  My body quick, my heart began to leap,
And every thorny thought did prick and sting,
  The fruit of my desirèd joys to reap;
    But he, on whom to think my soul still tires,
    In bale forsook and left me in the briars.

Thus fancy strung my lute to lays of love,
  And Love hath rock'd my weary muse asleep;
And sleep is broken by the pains I prove,
  And every pain I feel doth force me weep;
    Then farewell fancy, love, sleep, pain, and sore,
    And farewell weeping, I can wail no more.

Finis.   *Shep. Tony.*

PHYLLIDA'S LOVE-CALL TO HER

CORYDON, AND HIS REPLYING.

Phyl. CORYDON, arise, my Corydon!
              Titan shineth clear.
Cor.   Who is it that calleth Corydon?
              Who is it that I hear?

Phyl.   Phyllida, thy true love, calleth thee,
        Arise then, arise then ;
           Arise and keep thy flock with me !
Cor.   Phyllida, my true love, is it she ?
        I come then, I come then,
           I come and keep my flock with thee.

Phyl.   Here are cherries ripe for my Corydon ;
        Eat them for my sake.
Cor.   Here's my oaten pipe, my lovely one,
        Sport for thee to make.
Phyl.   Here are threads, my true love, fine as silk,
        To knit thee, to knit thee,
           A pair of stockings white as milk.
Cor.   Here are reeds, my true love, fine and neat,
        To make thee, to make thee,
           A bonnet to withstand the heat.

Phyl.   I will gather flowers, my Corydon,
        To set in thy cap.
Cor.   I will gather pears, my lovely one,
        To put in thy lap.
Phyl.   I will buy my true love garters gay,
        For Sundays, for Sundays,
           To wear about his legs so tall.
Cor.   I will buy my true love yellow say,
        For Sundays, for Sundays,
           To wear about her middle small.

Phyl.   When my Corydon sits on a hill
        Making melody—
Cor.   When my lovely one goes to her wheel,
        Singing cheerily—

Phyl.   Sure methinks my true love doth excel
    For sweetness, for sweetness,
     Our Pan, that old Arcadian knight.
Cor. And methinks my true love bears the bell
    For clearness, for clearness,
     Beyond the nymphs that be so bright.

Phyl. Had my Corydon, my Corydon,
    . Been, alack ! her [1] swain—
Cor. Had my lovely one, my lovely one,
    . Been in Ida plain—.
Phyl. Cynthia Endymion had refused,
    Preferring, preferring,
     My Corydon to play withal.
Cor. The queen of love had been excused
    Bequeathing, bequeathing,
     My Phyllida the golden ball.

Phyl. Yonder comes my mother, Corydon,
    Whither shall I fly ?
Cor. Under yonder beech, my lovely one,
    While she passeth by.
Phyl. Say to her thy true love was not here ;
    Remember, remember,
     To-morrow is another day.
Cor. Doubt me not, my true love, do not fear ;
    Farewell then, farewell then,
     Heaven keep our loves alway.
      Finis.   *Ignoto.*

---

[1] *England's Helicon,* " my."

THE SHEPHERD'S SOLACE.

PHŒBUS delights to view his laurel tree,
    The poplar pleaseth Hercules alone ;
Melissa mother is and fautrix to the bee,
    Pallas will wear the olive branch or none.[1]
      Of shepherds and their flocks Pales is queen,
      And Ceres ripes the corn was lately green.
To Chloris every flower belongs of right,
    The Dryad nymphs of woods make chief account ;
Oreades in hills have their delight,
    Diana doth protect each bubbling fount.
      To Hebe lovely kissing is assign'd,
      To Zephyr every gentle-breathing wind.
But what is Love's delight ? to hurt each where
    He cares not whom with darts of deep desire,
With watchful jealousy, with hope, with fear,
    With nipping cold, and secret flames of fire.
      O happy hour, wherein I did forego
      This little god, so great a cause of woe.
          Finis.   *Tho. Watson.*

SYRENUS' SONG TO EUGERIUS.

LET now the goodly springtide make us merry,
    And fields which pleasant flowers do adorn,
And vales, meads, woods, with lively colours flourish ;
Let plenteous flocks the shepherd's riches nourish ;

[1] "Or none" is the reading found in Watson's *Hecatom-pathia. England's Helicon* reads " alone."

Let hungry wolves by dogs to death be torn,
And lambs rejoice, with passèd winter weary;
 Let every river's ferry
In waters flow and silver streams abounding:
 And fortune, ceaseless wounding,
Turn now thy face, so cruel and unstable,
 Be firm and favourable;
And thou that kill'st our souls with thy pretences,
Molest not, wicked Love, my inward senses.

Let country plainness live in joys not ended;
 In quiet of the desert meads and mountains,
 And in the pleasure of a country dwelling,
Let shepherds rest, that have distillèd fountains
 Of tears; prove not thy wrath, all pains excelling,
 Upon poor souls, that never have offended.
  Let thy flames be incended
 In haughty courts, in those that swim in treasure,
  And live in ease and pleasure.
 And, that a sweetest scorn (my wonted sadness)
  A perfect rest and gladness,
 And hills and dales may give me, with offences
Molest not, wicked Love, my inward senses.

In what law find'st thou that the freest reason,
 And wit, unto thy chains should be subjected,
 And harmless souls unto thy cruel murder?
O wicked Love, the wretch that flieth furder
 From thy extremes, thou plagu'st.   O false,
  suspected,
 And careless boy, that thus thy sweets dost season!
  O vile and wicked treason,

Might not thy might suffice thee, but thy fuel
 Of force must be so cruel
To be a lord, yet like a tyrant minded,
 Vain boy, with error blinded?
Why dost thou hurt his life with thy offences,
That yields to thee his soul and inward senses?

He errs, alas! and foully is deceivèd,
 That calls thee god, being a burning fire,
 A furious flame, a plaining grief and clamorous;
And Venus' son (that in the earth was amorous,
 Gentle and mild and full of sweet desire,)
 Who calleth him, is of his wits bereavèd.
  And yet that she conceivèd
 By proof, so vile a son, and so unruly,
  I say (and yet say truly)
 That in the cause of harms, that they have framèd,
  Both justly may be blamèd;
 She that did breed him with such vile pretences,
 He that doth hurt so much our inward senses.

The gentle sheep and lambs are ever flying
 The ravenous wolves and beasts that are pretending
 To glut their maws with flesh they tear asunder.
The milk-white doves at noise of fearful thunder
 Fly home amain, themselves from harm defending;
 The little chick, when puttocks are a-crying,
  The woods and meadows dying
 For rain of heaven (if that they cannot have it)
  Do never cease to crave it.
 So everything his contrary resisteth,
  Only thy thrall persisteth
 In suffering of thy wrongs without offences,
 And lets thee spoil his heart and inward senses.

A public passion, Nature's laws restraining,
　And which with words can never be declarèd ;
　A soul 'twixt love, and fear, and desperation,
And endless plaint, that shuns all consolation ;
　A spendless flame, that never is impairèd,
　A friendless death, yet life in death maintaining ;
　　A passion, that is gaining
On him that loveth well, and is absented,
　Whereby it is augmented ;
　A jealousy, a burning grief and sorrow,—
　　These favours lovers borrow
Of thee, fell Love ; these be thy recompenses,
Consuming still their soul and inward senses.
　　　　　　Finis.　　　　*Bar. Young.*

THE SHEPHERD ARSILIUS' REPLY TO SYRENUS' SONG.

O LET that time a thousand months endure,
　　Which brings from heaven the sweet and silver
　　　showers,
And joys the earth (of comfort late deprived)
　With grass and leaves, fine buds and painted flowers.
　Echo, return unto the woods obscure,
　Ring forth the shepherds' songs in love contrived,
　　Let old loves be revived,
　Which angry winter buried but of late,
　　And that in such a state
My soul may have the full accomplishment
　　Of joy and sweet content :
And since fierce pains and griefs thou dost control,
Good Love, do not forsake my inward soul.

Presume not, shepherds, once to make you merry
With springs, and flowers, or any pleasant song,
Unless mild Love possess your amorous breasts ;
  If you sing not to him, your songs do weary ; '
  Crown him with flowers, or else ye do him wrong ;
  And consecrate your springs to his behests.
     I to my shepherdess
  My happy loves with great content do sing,
    And flowers to her do bring,
  And sitting near her by the river-side,
    Enjoy the brave springtide.
  Since then thy joys such sweetness doth enroll,
  Good Love, do not forsake my inward soul.

The wise (in ancient times) a god thee named,
Seeing that with thy power and supreme might,
Thou didst such rare and mighty wonders make ;
  For thee a heart is frozen and enflamed,
  A fool thou mak'st a wise man with thy light,
  The coward turns courageous for thy sake ;
     The mighty gods did quake
  At thy command ; to birds and beasts transform'd,
    Great monarchs have not scorn'd
  To yield unto the force of beauty's lure ;
    Such spoils thou dost procure
  With thy brave force, which never may be told,
  With which, sweet Love, thou conquer'st every soul.

In other times obscurely I did live,
But with a drowsy, base, and simple kind
Of life, and only to my profit bend me ;
  To think of love myself I did not give,
  Or for good grace, good parts, and gentle mind,

H

Never did any shepherdess commend me :
    But crownèd now they send me
A thousand garlands, that I won with praise,
    In wrestling days by days,
In pitching of the bar with arm most strong,
    And singing many a song,
After that thou didst honour and take hold
    Of my sweet love and of my happy soul.

What greater joy can any man desire
Than to remain a captive unto Love,
And have his heart subjected to his power ?
    And though sometimes he taste a little sour
    By suffering it, as mild as gentle dove
    Yet must he be, in lieu of that great hire
        Whereto he doth aspire ;
    If lovers live afflicted and in pain,
        Let them with cause complain
    Of cruel fortune, and of time's abuse,
        And let not them accuse
    Thee, gentle Love, that doth with bliss enfold
    Within thy sweetest joys each living soul.

Behold a fair sweet face, and shining eyes
Resembling two most bright and twinkling stars,
Sending unto the soul a perfect light ;
    Behold the rare perfections of those white
    And ivory hands from grief's most surest bars ;
    That mind wherein all life and glory lies,
        That joy that never dies,
    That he doth feel that loves and is beloved ;
        And my delights approved,

To see her pleased, whose love maintains me here ;
    All those I count so dear,
That though sometimes love doth my joys control,
Yet I am glad he dwells within my soul.

                Finis.   *Bar. Young.*

A SHEPHERD'S DREAM.

A SILLY shepherd lately sat
    Among a flock of sheep ;
Where musing long on this and that,
    At last he fell asleep.
And in the slumber as he lay,
    He gave a piteous groan ;
He thought his sheep were run away,
    And he was left alone.
He whoop'd, he whistled, and he call'd,
    But not a sheep came near him ;
Which made the shepherd sore appall'd
    To see that none would hear him.
But as the swain amazèd stood,
    In this most solemn vein,
Came Phyllida forth of the wood,
    And stood before the swain.
Whom when the shepherd did behold,
    He straight began to weep,
And at the heart he grew a-cold,
    To think upon his sheep.
For well he knew, where came the queen,
    The shepherd durst not stay :

And where that he durst not be seen,
    The sheep must needs away.
To ask her if she saw his flock,
    Might happen patience move,
And have an answer with a mock,
    That such demanders prove.
Yet for because he saw her come
    Alone out of the wood,
He thought he would not stand as dumb,
    When speech might do him good ;
And therefore falling on his knees,
    To ask but for his sheep,
He did awake, and so did leese
    The honour of his sleep.
                    Finis.   *N. Breton.*

THE SHEPHERD'S ODE.

NIGHTS were short and days were long,
    Blossoms on the hawthorn hong,
Philomel, night-music's king,
Told the coming of the Spring.
Whose sweet silver-sounding voice
Made the little birds rejoice,
Skipping light from spray to spray,
Till Aurora show'd the day..
Scarce might one see, when I might see
(For such chances sudden be)
By a well of marble-stone,
A shepherd lying all alone.

Weep he did, and his weeping
Made the fading flowers spring.
Daphnis was his name I ween,
Youngest swain of summer's queen.
When Aurora saw 'twas he,
Weep she did for company ;
Weep she did for her sweet son,
That (when antique Troy was won)
Suffer'd death by luckless fate,
Whom she now laments too late,
And each morning (by cock's crew)
Showers down her silver dew,
Whose tears falling from their spring,
Give moisture to each living thing
That on earth increase and grow,
Through power of their friendly foe.
Whose effect when Flora felt,
Tears, that did her bosom melt,
(For who can resist tears often,
But she whom no tears can soften ?)
Peering straight above the banks,
Show'd herself to give her thanks,
Wond'ring thus at Nature's work
(Wherein many marvels lurk).
Methought I heard a doleful noise
Consorted with a mournful voice ;
Drawing near, to hear more plain,
Hear I did, unto my pain,
(For who is not pain'd to hear
Him in grief whom heart holds dear ?)
Silly swain with grief o'er-gone,
Thus to make his piteous moan :—
" Love I did, alas ! the while,

Love I did, but did beguile
My dear love with loving so,
Whom as then I did not know.
Love I did the fairest boy
That these fields did e'er enjoy ;
Love I did fair Ganymede,
Venus' darling, beauty's bed ;
Him I thought the fairest creature,
Him the quintessence of nature.
But yet, alas ! I was deceived,
(Love of reason is bereaved,)
For since then I saw a lass,
Lass that did in beauty pass,
Pass fair Ganymede as far
As Phœbus doth the smallest star.
Love commanded me to love,
Fancy bade me not remove
My affection from the swain
Whom I never could obtain.
(For who can obtain that favour
Which he cannot grant the craver ?)
Love at last, though loth, prevail'd,
Love that so my heart assail'd,
Wounding me with her fair eyes :
Ah, how Love can subtilize,
And devise a thousand shifts
How to work men to his drifts !
Her it is for whom I mourn,
Her for whom my life I scorn ;
Her for whom I weep all day,
Her for whom I sigh and say,
Either she, or else no creature,
Shall enjoy my love ; whose feature

Though I never can obtain,
Yet shall my true love remain,
Till (my body turn'd to clay)
My poor soul must pass away
To the heavens ; where I hope
It shall find a resting scope:
Then since I loved thee alone,
Remember me when I am gone."
Scarce had he these last words spoken,
But methought his heart was broken,
With great grief that did abound,
(Cares and grief the heart confound,)
In whose heart, thus rived in three,
Eliza written I might see
In characters of crimson blood,
Whose meaning well I understood;
Which for my heart might not behold,
I hied me home my sheep to fold.

        Finis.   *Rich. Barnefield.*

THE SHEPHERD'S COMMENDATION OF

HIS NYMPH.

WHAT shepherd can express
    The favour of her face,
To whom in this distress
I do appeal for grace ?
    A thousand Cupids fly
    About her gentle eye.

From which each throws a dart
That kindleth soft sweet fire
Within my sighing heart,
Possessèd by desire;
    No sweeter life I try
    Than in her love to die.

The lily in the field,
That glories in his white,
For pureness now must yield,
And render up his right;
    Heaven pictured in her face
    Doth promise joy and grace.

Fair Cynthia's silver light,
That beats on running streams,
Compares not with her white,
Whose hairs are all sunbeams.
    So bright my nymph doth shine
    As day unto my eyne.

With this there is a red,
Exceeds the damask-rose,
Which in her cheeks is spread,
Where every favour grows;
    In sky there is no star,
    But she surmounts it far.

When Phœbus from the bed
Of Thetis doth arise,
The morning blushing red,
In fair carnation-wise, :
    He shows in my nymph's face,
    As queen of every grace.

This pleasant lily white,
This taint of roseate red,
This Cynthia's silver light,
This sweet fair Dea spread,
　　These sunbeams in mine eye,
　　These beauties make me die.
　　　　Finis.　　*Earl of Oxenford.*

CORYDON TO HIS PHYLLIS.

ALAS ! my heart, mine eye hath wrongèd thee,
　　Presumptuous eye, to gaze on Phyllis' face,
Whose heavenly eye no mortal man may see,
But he must die or purchase Phyllis' grace.
　　Poor Corydon, the nymph whose eye doth move thee,
　　Doth love to draw, but is not drawn to love thee.
Her beauty, Nature's pride and shepherds' praise ;
Her eye, the heavenly planet of my life ;
Her matchless wit and grace her fame displays,
As if that Jove had made her for his wife :
　　Only her eyes shoot fiery darts to kill,
　　Yet is her heart as cold as Caucase hill.
My wings too weak to fly against the sun,
Mine eyes unable to sustain her light ;
My heart doth yield that I am quite undone,
Thus hath fair Phyllis slain me with her sight ;
　　My bud is blasted, wither'd is my leaf,
　　And all my corn is rotted in the sheaf.
Phyllis, the golden fetter of my mind,
My fancy's idol and my vital power,

Goddess of nymphs and honour of thy kind,
This age's phœnix, beauty's richest bower,
  Poor Corydon for love of thee must die,
  Thy beauty's thrall and conquest of thine eye.
Leave, Corydon, to plough the barren field,
Thy buds of hope are blasted with disgrace ;
For Phyllis' looks no hearty love do yield,
Nor can she love, for all her lovely face.
  Die, Corydon, the spoil of Phyllis' eye ;
  She cannot love, and therefore thou must die.
                    Finis.   *S. E. Dyer.*

THE SHEPHERD'S DESCRIPTION OF
LOVE.

Melibœus. SHEPHERD, what's Love, I pray thee
                  tell?
Faustus.   It is that fountain and that well,
             Where pleasure and repentance dwell ;
             It is perhaps that sauncing bell,
                 That tolls all in to heaven or hell :
                 And this is Love, as I heard tell.
Meli.   Yet what is Love, I prithee say?
Faust.   It is a work on holiday,
             It is December match'd with May,
             When lusty bloods in fresh array
                 Hear ten months after of the play :
                 And this is Love, as I hear say.
Meli.   Yet what is Love, good shepherd, sain?
Faust.   It is a sunshine mix'd with rain,

It is a tooth-ache, or like pain,
It is a game, where none doth gain ;
    The lass saith no, and would full fain :
    And this is Love, as I hear sain.

Meli. Yet, shepherd, what is Love, I pray ?
Faust. It is a yea, it is a nay,
A pretty kind of sporting fray,
It is a thing will soon away,
    Then, nymphs, take vantage while ye may :
    And this is Love, as I hear say,

Meli. Yet what is Love, good shepherd, show ?
Faust. A thing that creeps, it cannot go,
A prize that passeth to and fro,
A thing for one, a thing for moe,
    And he that proves shall find it so :
    And, shepherd, this is Love, I trow.
           Finis.   *Ignoto.*

TO HIS FLOCKS.

FEED on, my flocks, securely,
    Your shepherd watcheth surely ;
Run about, my little lambs,
Skip and wanton with your dams,
    Your loving herd with care will tend ye.
Sport on, fair flocks, at pleasure,
Nip Vesta's flow'ring treasure ;
I myself will duly hark,
When my watchful dog doth bark ;
    From wolf and fox I will defend ye.
           Finis.   *H. C.*

A ROUNDELAY BETWEEN TWO
SHEPHERDS.

1 *Shep.* TELL me, thou gentle shepherd swain,
         Who's yonder in the vale is set?
2 *Shep.* Oh, it is she, whose sweets do stain
         The lily, rose, the violet!

1 *Shep.* Why doth the sun against his kind
         Fix his bright chariot in the skies?
2 *Shep.* Because the sun is stricken blind
         With looking on her heavenly eyes.

1 *Shep.* Why do thy flocks forbear their food,
         Which sometime were thy chief delight?
2 *Shep.* Because they need no other good
         That live in presence of her sight.

1 *Shep.* Why look these flowers so pale and ill,
         That once attired this goodly heath?
2 *Shep.* She hath robb'd Nature of her skill,
         And sweetens all things with her breath.

1 *Shep.* Why slide these brooks so slow away,
         Whose bubbling murmur pleased thine ear?
2 *Shep.* Oh, marvel not although they stay,
         When they her heavenly voice do hear!

1 *Shep.* From whence come all these shepherd swains,
         And lovely nymphs attired in green?
2 *Shep.* From gathering garlands on the plains,
         To crown our fair the shepherds' queen.

Both. The sun that lights this world below,
    Flocks, flowers, and brooks will witness bear:
    These nymphs and shepherds all do know,
    That it is she is only fair.
                Finis.   *Michael Drayton.*

THE SOLITARY SHEPHERD'S SONG.

O SHADY vales, O fair enrichèd meads,
    O sacred woods, sweet fields, and rising
        mountains;
O painted flowers, green herbs where Flora treads,
    Refresh'd by wanton winds and wat'ry fountains.

O all you wingèd choristers of wood,
    That perch'd aloft your former pains report,
And straight again recount with pleasant mood
    Your present joys in sweet and seemly sort.

O all you creatures whosoever thrive,
    On mother earth, in seas, by air, by fire,
More blest are you than I here under sun:
    Love dies in me, whenas he doth revive
In you; I perish under beauty's ire,
    Where after storms, winds, frosts, your life is won.
              Finis.   *Thom. Lodge.*

THE SHEPHERD'S RESOLUTION IN LOVE.

IF Jove himself be subject unto Love,
    And range the woods to find a mortal prey ;
If Neptune from the seas himself remove,
And seek on sands with earthly wights to play :
    Then may I love my shepherdess [1] by right,
    Who far excels each other mortal wight ?

If Pluto could by Love be drawn from hell
To yield himself a silly virgin's thrall ;
If Phœbus could vouchsafe on earth to dwell,
To win a rustic maid unto his call :
    Then how much more should I adore the sight
    Of her in whom the heavens themselves delight ?

If country Pan might follow nymphs in chase,
And yet through Love remain devoid of blame ;
If satyrs were excused for seeking grace
To joy the fruits of any mortal dame :
    My [2] shepherdess, why should not I love still,
    On whom nor gods nor men can gaze their fill ?

                    Finis.   *Thom. Watson.*

[1] For "Shepherdess" Watson's *Hecatompathia* reads "peer-
lesse choice."

[2] Watson's *Hecatompathia* reads "Then why should I once
doubt to love her still."

CORYDON'S HYMN IN PRAISE OF
AMARYLLIS.

WOULD mine eyes were crystal fountains,
    Where you might the shadow view
Of my griefs, like to these mountains,
Swelling for the loss of you !
Cares which cureless are, alas !
Helpless, hapless, for they grow ;
Cares like tares in number pass
All the seeds that Love doth sow.
Who but could remember all ?
Twinkling eyes still representing
Stars which pierce me to the gall,
'Cause they lend no more contenting.
And you, nectar-lips, alluring
Human sense to taste of heaven ;
For no art of man's manuring
Finer silk hath ever weaven.
Who but could remember this ?
The sweet odours of your favour
When I smell'd I was in bliss,
Never felt I sweeter savour.
And your harmless heart anointed,
As the custom was of kings,
Shows your sacred soul appointed
To be prime of earthly things.
Ending thus remember all :
Clothèd in a mantle green ;—
'Tis-enough I am your thrall ;

Leave to think what eye hath seen.
Yet the eye may not so leave,
Though the thought do still repine,
But must gaze till death bequeath
Eyes and thoughts unto her shrine.
Which if Amaryllis chance
Hearing to make haste to see,
To life death she may advance :
Therefore eyes and thoughts goes free.
                    Finis.   *T. B.*

THE SHEPHERD CARILLO HIS SONG.

GUARDA mi las Vaccas
  Carillo, por tu fe.
Besa mi primero,
  Yo te las guardare.
"I prithee keep my kine for me,
  Carillo, wilt thou ? Tell."
"First let me have a kiss of thee,
  And I will keep them well."

"If to my charge, or them to keep;
Thou dost commend thy kine or sheep,
  For thee I do suffice,
Because in this I have been bred ;
But for so much as I have fed,
  By viewing thee, mine eyes,
  Command not me to keep thy beast,
  Because myself I can keep least.

How can I keep, I prithee tell,
Thy kie, myself that cannot well
   Defend, nor please thy kind,
As long as I have servèd thee?
But if thou wilt give unto me
   A kiss to please my mind,
  I ask no more for all my pain,
  And I will keep them very fain.

For thee, the gift is not so great
That I do ask, to keep thy neat,
   But unto me it is
A guerdon that shall make me live.
Disdain not then to lend, or give,
   So small a gift as this.
  But if to it thou canst not frame,
  Then give me leave to take the same.

But if thou dost, my sweet, deny
To recompense me by-and-by,
   Thy promise shall relent me ;
Hereafter some reward to find,
Behold how I do please my mind,
   And favours do content me.
  That though thou speak'st it but in jest,
  I mean to take it at the best.

Behold how much love works in me,
And how ill recompensed of thee ;
   That with the shadow of
Thy happy favours (though delay'd)
I think myself right well appay'd.
   Although they prove a scoff.

I

Then pity me that have forgot,
Myself for thee that carest not.

Oh, in extreme thou art most fair,
And in extreme unjust despair
    Thy cruelty maintains ;
Oh, that thou wert so pitiful
Unto these torments that do pull
    My soul with senseless pains,
    As thou show'st in that face of thine,
    Where pity and mild grace should shine.

If that thy fair and sweetest face
Assureth me both peace and grace,
    Thy hard and cruel heart,
Which in that white breast thou dost bear,
Doth make me tremble yet for fear
    Thou wilt not end my smart.
    In contraries of such a kind,
    Tell me what succour shall I find?

If then, young shepherdess, thou crave
A herdsman for thy beast to have,
    With grace thou mayst restore
Thy shepherd from his barren love,
For never other shalt thou prove,
    That seeks to please thee more ;
    And who, to serve thy turn, will never shun
    The nipping frost and beams of parching sun."

        Finis.   *Bar. Young.*

CORIN'S DREAM OF HIS FAIR CHLORIS.

WHAT time bright Titan in the zenith sat
　　And equally the fixèd poles did heat,
When to my flock my daily woes I chat,
And underneath a broad beech took my seat,
The dreaming god, which Morpheus poets call,
Augmenting fuel to my Etna's fire,
With sleep possessing my weak senses all,
In apparitions makes my hopes aspire.
Methought I saw the nymph I would embrace,
With arms abroad coming to me for help ;
A lust-led satyr having her in chase,
Which after her about the fields did yelp.
I seeing my love in such perplexèd plight,
A sturdy bat from off an oak I reft,
And with the ravisher continued fight,
Till breathless I upon the earth him left,
Then when my coy nymph saw her breathless foe,
With kisses kind she gratifies my pain ;
Protesting rigour never more to show.
Happy was I this good hap to obtain ;
But drowsy slumbers flying to their cell,
My sudden joy converted was to bale.
My wonted sorrows still with me do dwell ;
I lookèd round about on hill and dale,
But I could neither my fair Chloris view,
Nor yet the satyr which erewhile I slew.

　　　　　Finis.　　　　　　*W. S.*

THE SHEPHERD DAMON'S PASSION.

AH trees, why fall your leaves so fast?
    Ah rocks, where are your robes of moss?
Ah flocks, why stand you all aghast?
Trees, rocks, and flocks, what are ye pensive for my
    loss?

The birds methinks tune nought but moan,
The winds breathe nought but bitter plaint,
The beasts forsake their dens to groan :
Birds, winds, and beasts, what doth my loss your
    powers attaint?

Floods weep their springs above their bounds,
And echo wails to see my woe,
The robe of ruth doth clothe the grounds :
Floods, echo, grounds, why do ye all these tears
    bestow?

The trees, the rocks, and flocks reply,
The birds, the winds, the beasts report,
Floods, echo, grounds for sorrow cry,
" We grieve since Phyllis nill kind Damon's love
    consort."

                Finis.   *Thom. Lodge.*

THE SHEPHERD MUSIDORUS HIS COMPLAINT.

COME, shepherds' weeds, become your master's
　　mind,
Yield outward show, what inward change[1] he tries ;
Nor be abash'd since such a guest you find,
Whose strongest hope in your weak comfort lies.
Come, shepherds' weeds, attend my woful cries,
Disuse yourselves from sweet Menalcas' voice ;
For other be those tunes which sorrow ties,
From those clear notes which freely may rejoice.
　　Then pour out plaint, and in one word say this,—
　　Helpless his plaints who spoils himself of bliss.

　　　　　　　Finis.　　*Sir Phil. Sidney.*

THE SHEPHERDS' BRAWL, ONE HALF ANSWERING THE OTHER.

1.　WE love, and have our loves rewarded.
2.　　　We love, and are no whit regarded.
1.　We find most sweet affection's snare.
2.　That sweet but sour despairful care.
1.　Who can despair whom hope doth bear?
2.　And who can hope that feels despair?
All.　As without breath no pipe doth move,
　　　No music kindly without love.

　　　　　　　Finis.　　*Sir Phil. Sidney.*

[1] The 1590 *Arcadia*, p. 77 (where these verses first appeared),
reads "chance."

DORUS HIS COMPARISONS.

M Y sheep are thoughts which I both guide and
        serve,
Their pasture is fair hills of fruitless love ;
On barren sweets they feed, and feeding sterve,
I wail their lot, but will not other prove.
My sheep-hook is wan hope, which all upholds ;
My weeds, desires, cut out in endless folds.
    What wool my sheep shall bear, while thus they live,
    In you it is, you must the judgment give.
                    Finis.   Sir Phil. Sidney.

THE SHEPHERD FAUSTUS HIS SONG.

A fair maid wed to prying Jealousy,
One of the fairest as ever I did see ;
If that thou wilt a secret lover take,
Sweet life, do not my secret love forsake.

E CLIPSED was our sun,
    And fair Aurora darken'd to us quite ;
Our morning star was done,
    And shepherd's star lost clean out of our sight,
    When that thou didst thy faith in wedlock plight.

Dame Nature made thee fair,
  And ill did careless fortune marry thee,
And pity with despair
  It was, that this thy hapless hap should be,
  A fair maid wed to prying Jealousy.

Our eyes are not so bold
  To view the sun, that flies with radiant wing,
Unless that we do hold
  A glass before them, or some other thing.
  Then wisely this to pass did fortune bring
To cover thee with such a veil ;
  For heretofore when any viewèd thee,
Thy sight made his to fail.
  Forsooth thou art, thy beauty telleth me,
  One of the fairest as ever I did see.

Thy graces to obscure
  With such a froward husband, and so base,
She meant thereby most sure
  That Cupid's force and love thou shouldst embrace,
  For 'tis a force to love, no wondrous case ;
Then care no more for kin,
  And doubt no more for fear thou must forsake.
To love thou must begin ;
  And from henceforth this question never make,
  If that thou shouldst a secret lover take.

Of force it doth behove
  That thou shouldst be beloved, and that again,
Fair mistress, thou shouldst love ;
  For to what end, what purpose, and what gain,
  Should such perfections serve, as now in vain ?

My love is of such art,
  That (of itself) it well deserves to take
In thy sweet love a part :
  Then for no shepherd, that his love doth make,
  Sweet life, do not my secret love forsake.   ·
                     Finis.   *Bar. Young.*

ANOTHER OF THE SAME, BY FIRMIUS

THE SHEPHERD.

IF that the gentle wind
  Doth move the leaves with pleasant sound,
If that the kid behind
Is left, that cannot find
  Her dam, runs bleating up and down ;
The bagpipe, reed, or flute,
  Only with air if that they touchèd be,
With pity all salute,
And full of love do bruit
  Thy name, and sound Diana, seeing thee
  A fair maid wed to prying Jealousy.

The fierce and savage beasts
  (Beyond their kind and nature yet)
With piteous voice and breast,
In mountains without rest,
  The self-same song do not forget.
If that they stay'd at *fair*
  And had not pass'd to *prying Jealousy*

With plaints of such despair,
As moved the gentle air
  To tears ; the song that they did sing should be,
  One of the fairest as ever I did see.

Mishap, and fortune's play,
  Ill did they place in beauty's breast ;
For since so much to say
There was of beauty's sway,
  They had done well to leave the rest.
They had enough to do,
  If in her praise their wits they did awake ;
But yet so must they too,
And all thy love that woo
  Thee not too coy, nor too too proud to make,
  If that thou wilt a secret lover take.

For if thou hadst but known
  The beauty that they here do touch,
Thou wouldst then love alone
Thyself, nor any one,
  Only thyself accounting much.
But if thou dost conceive
  This beauty, that I will not public make,
And mean'st not to bereave
The world of it, but leave
  The same to some (which never peer did take),
  Sweet life, do not my secret love forsake.
                    Finis.   *Bar. Young.*

DAMELUS' SONG TO HIS DIAPHENIA.

DIAPHENIA, like the daffadowndilly,
  White as the sun, fair as the lily,
Heigho, how I do love thee !
I do love thee as my lambs
Are belovèd of their dams :
  How blest were I if thou wouldst prove me !

Diaphenia, like the spreading roses,
That in thy sweets all sweets encloses,
  Fair sweet, how I do love thee !
I do love thee as each flower
Loves the sun's life-giving power ;
  For dead, thy breath to life might move me.

Diaphenia, like to all things blessèd,
When all thy praises are expressèd,
  Dear joy, how I do love thee !
As the birds do love the Spring,
Or the bees their careful king :
  Then in requite, sweet virgin, love me !

Finis.   *H. C.*

THE SHEPHERD EURYMACHUS TO HIS

FAIR SHEPHERDESS MIRIMIDA.

WHEN Flora, proud in pomp of all her flowers,
    Sat bright and gay,
And gloried in the dew of Iris' showers,
    And did display

Her mantle chequer'd all with gaudy green ;
      Then I
      Alone
A mournful man in Erecyne was seen.

With folded arms I trampled through the grass,
      Tracing as he
That held the throne of Fortune brittle glass,
      And Love to be,
Like Fortune, fleeting as the restless wind
      Mixèd
      'With mists,
Whose damp doth make the clearest eyes grow blind.

Thus in a maze, I spied a hideous flame ;
      I cast my sight,
And saw where, blithely bathing in the same,
      With great delight
A worm did lie, wrapt in a smoky sweat :
      And yet
      'Twas strange,
It careless lay and shrunk not at the heat.

I stood amazed and wond'ring at the sight,
      While that a dame,
That shone like to the heaven's rich sparkling light,
      Discoursed the same,
And said, "My friend, this worm within the fire
      Which lies
      Content,
Is Venus' worm, and represents desire.

" A salamander is this princely beast,
    Deck'd with a crown,
Given him by Cupid as a gorgeous crest
    'Gainst Fortune's frown.
Content he lies, and bathes him in the flame,
    And goes
    Not forth,
For why he cannot live without the same.

" As he, so lovers live within the fire
    Of fervent love,
And shrink not from the flame of hot desire,
    Nor will not move
From any heat that Venus' force imparts,
    But lie
    Content
Within a fire, and waste away their hearts."

Up flew the dame, and vanish'd in a cloud :
    But there stood I,
And many thoughts within my mind did shroud
    My[1] love ; for why
I felt within my heart a scorching fire,
    And yet
    As did
The salamander, 'twas my whole desire.
         Finis.   *Ro. Greene.*

[1] In Greene's *Francesco's Fortunes, or the Second Part of Never too Late,* 1590 (whence the poem is taken), the reading is " Of love."

THE SHEPHERD FIRMIUS HIS SONG.

SHEPHERDS, give ear, and now be still,
 Unto my passions and their cause,
  And what they be;
Since that with such an earnest will
And such great signs of friendship's laws,
  You ask it me.

It is not long since I was whole,
Nor since I did in every part
  Free-will resign;
It is not long since in my sole
Possession I did know my heart,
  And to be mine.

It is not long since, even and morrow,
All pleasure that my heart could find
  Was in my power;
It is not long since grief and sorrow
My loving heart began to bind,
  And to devour.

It is not long since company
I did esteem a joy indeed
  Still to frequent;
Nor long, since solitarily
I lived and that this life did breed
  My sole content.

Desirous I (wretched) to see,
But thinking not to see so much
    As then I saw ;
Love made me know in what degree
His valour and brave force did touch
    Me with his law.

First he did put no more nor less
Into my heart than he did view
    That there did want ;
But when my breast in such excess
Of lively flames to burn I knew,
    Then were so scant

My joys, that now did so abate,
(Myself estrangèd every way
    From former rest)
That I did know that my estate,
And that my life, was every day
    In Death's arrest.

I put my hand into my side
To see what was the cause of this
    Unwonted vein,
Where I did find that torments lied
By endless death to prejudice
    My life with pain.

Because I saw that there did want
My heart, wherein I did delight,
    My dearest heart ;
And he that did the same supplant
No jurisdiction had of right
    To play that part.

The judge and robber that remain
Within my soul, their cause to try,
 Are there all one ;
And so the giver of the pain,
And he that is condemn'd to die,
 Or I, or none.

To die I care not any way,
Though without why, to die I grieve,
 As I do see ;
But for because I heard her say,
" None die for love, for I believe
 None such there be."

Then this thou shalt believe by me
Too late, and without remedy,
 As did in brief
Anaxarete, and thou shalt see
The little she did satisfy
 With after grief.

   Finis. *Bar. Young.*

THE SHEPHERD'S PRAISE OF HIS
SACRED DIANA.

PRAISED be Diana's fair and harmless light,
 Praised be the dews wherewith she moists the
  ground,
Praised be her beams, the glory of the night,
 Praised be her power, by which all powers abound.

Praised be her nymphs, with whom she decks the
    woods,
Praised be her knights, in whom true honour lives,
Praised be that force by which she moves the floods ;
    Let that Diana shine which all these gives !

In heaven queen she is among the spheres,
She mistress-like makes all things to be pure ;
Eternity in her oft change she bears ;
    She beauty is, by her the fair endure.

Time wears her not, she doth his chariot guide ;
Mortality below her orb is placed ;
By her the virtue of the stars down slide,
    In her is virtue's perfect image cast.

A knowledge pure it is her worth to know ;
With Circes let them dwell that think not so.
                Finis.   *Ignoto.*

THE SHEPHERD'S DUMP.

LIKE desert woods, with darksome shades obscurèd,
    Where dreadful beasts, where hateful horror
    reigneth,
  Such is my wounded heart, whom sorrow paineth.

The trees are fatal shafts, to death inurèd,
That cruel love within my heart maintaineth
  To whet my grief, whenas my sorrow waneth.

The ghastly beasts, my thoughts in cares assurèd,
Which wage me war, whilst heart no succour gaineth,
  With false suspect and fear that still remaineth.

The horrors, burning sighs, by cares procurèd,
Which forth I send, whilst weeping eye complaineth,
  To cool the heat the helpless heart containeth.

But shafts, but cares, sighs, horrors unrecurèd,
Were nought esteem'd if, for their pains awarded,
  Your shepherd's love might be by you regarded.
                    Finis.   *S. E. D.*

THE NYMPH DIANA'S SONG.

WHEN that I, poor soul, was born,
    I was born unfortunate ;
Presently the fates had sworn,
To foretell my hapless state.

Titan his fair beams did hide,
Phœbe 'clipsed her silver light ;
In my birth my mother died,
Young and fair in heavy plight.

And the nurse that gave me suck,
Hapless was in all her life ;
And I never had good luck,
Being maid or married wife.

K

I loved well, and was beloved,
And forgetting, was forgot ;
This a hapless marriage moved,
Grieving that it kills me not.

With the earth would I were wed,
Than in such a grave of woes
Daily to be burièd,
Which no end nor number knows.

Young my father married me,
Forced by my obedience ;
Sirenus, thy faith and thee
I forgot without offence.

Which contempt I pay so far,
Never like was paid so much ;
Jealousies do make me war,
But without a cause of such.

I do go with jealous eyes,
To my folds and to my sheep ;
And with jealousy I rise,
When the day begins to peep.

At his table I do eat,
In his bed with him I lie ;
But I take no rest nor meat,
Without cruel jealousy.

If I ask him what he ails,
And whereof he jealous is,
In his answer then he fails,
Nothing can he say to this.

In his face there is no cheer,
But he ever hangs the head ;
In each corner he doth peer,
And his speech is sad and dead.

    Ill the poor soul lives, I wis,
    That so hardly married is.
        Finis.   *Bar. Young.*

ROWLAND'S MADRIGAL.

FAIR Love, rest thee here,
   Never yet was morn so clear ;
Sweet, be not unkind,
Let me thy favour find,
   Or else for love I die.
Hark this pretty bubbling spring,
How it makes the meadows ring !
Love, now stand my friend,
Here let all sorrow end,
   And I will honour thee.
  See where little Cupid lies,
  Looking babies in her eyes !
  Cupid, help me now,
  Lend to me thy bow,
    To wound her that wounded me.
  Here is none to see or tell,
  All our flocks are feeding by ;
  This bank with roses spread,
  Oh, it is a dainty bed,
    Fit for my love and me.

Hark the birds in yonder grove,
How they chant unto my love !
Love, be kind to me,
As I have been to thee,
    For thou hast won my heart.
Calm winds, blow you fair,
Rock her, thou sweet gentle air ;
Oh, the morn is noon,
The evening comes too soon,
    To part my love and me.
  The roses and thy lips do meet ;
  Oh, that life were half so sweet !
  Who would respect his breath,
  That might die such a death ?
      Oh, that life thus might die !
All the bushes that be near,
With sweet nightingales beset :
Hush, sweet ! and be still,
Let them sing their fill,
      There's none our joys to let.

Sun, why dost thou go so fast ?
Oh, why dost thou make such haste ?
It is too early yet,
So soon from joys to flit.
    Why art thou so unkind ?
See my little lambkins run,
Look on them till I have done ;
Haste not on the night,
To rob me of her sight,
    That live but by her eyes.
  Alas ! sweet love, we must depart ;
  Hark, my dog begins to bark !

Somebody's coming near ;
They shall not find us here,
　　For fear of being chid.
Take my garland and my glove,
Wear it for my sake, my love.
To-morrow on the green,
Thou shalt be our shepherds' queen,
　　Crown'd with roses gay.

　　　　　Finis.　Michael Drayton.

ALANIUS THE SHEPHERD HIS DOLEFUL SONG, COMPLAINING OF ISMENIA'S CRUELTY.

NO more, O cruel nymph ! now hast thou prey'd
　　Enough in thy revenge ; prove not thine ire
On him that yields ; the fault is now appay'd
Unto my cost ; now mollify thy dire
Hardness, and breast of thine so much obdured,
And now raise up (though lately it hath err'd)
A poor repenting soul, that in the obscured
Darkness of thy oblivion lies interr'd :
　　For it falls not in that, that should commend thee,
　　That such a swain as I may once offend thee.

If that the little sheep with speed is flying
From angry shepherd (with his words afraid),
And runneth here and there with fearful crying,
And with great grief is from the flock estray'd ;

But when it now perceives that none doth follow,
And all alone so far estraying mourneth,
Knowing what danger it is in, with hollow
And fainting bleats ; then fearful it returneth
    Unto the flock, meaning no more to leave it,—
    Should it not be a just thing to receive it ?

Lift up those eyes, Ismenia, which so stately,
To view me, thou hast lifted up before me ;
That liberty which was mine own but lately,
Give me again, and to the same restore me ;
And that mild heart, so full of love and pity,
Which thou didst yield to me, and ever owe me :
Behold, my nymph, I was not then so witty
To know that sincere love that thou didst show me :
    Now, woful man, full well I know and rue it,
    Although it was too late before I knew it.

How could it be, my enemy, say, tell me,
How thou (in greater fault and error being
Than ever I was thought) shouldst thus repel me?
And with new league and cruel title seeing
Thy faith so pure and worthy to be changèd?
And what is that, Ismenia, that doth bind it
To love, whereas the same is most estrangèd,
And where it is impossible to find it ?
    But pardon me, if herein I abuse thee :
    Since that the cause thou gav'st me doth excuse me.

But tell me now, what honour hast thou gainèd,
Avenging such a fault by thee committed,
And thereunto by thy occasion trainèd ?
What have I done, that I have not acquitted?

Or what excess that is not amply payèd,
Or suffer more, than I have not endurèd?
What cruel mind, what angry breast displayèd
With savage heart, to fierceness so adjurèd?
    Would not such mortal grief make mild and tender,
    But that which my fell shepherdess doth render?

Now as I have perceivèd well thy reasons,
Which thou hast had, or hast yet, to forget me,
The pains, the griefs, the guilts of forcèd treasons,
That I have done, wherein thou first didst set me,
The passions, and thrine ears' and eyes' refusing
To peer and see me, meaning to undo me:
Cam'st thou to know, or be but once perusing,
Th' unsought occasions, which thou gav'st unto me,
    Thou shouldst not have wherewith to 'more
        torment me,
    Nor I to pay the fault my rashness lent me.
                    Finis.   *Bar. Young.*

MONTANA THE SHEPHERD HIS LOVE

TO AMINTA.

I SERVE Aminta, whiter than the snow,
    Straighter than cedar, brighter than the glass;
More fine in trip than foot of running roe,
More pleasant than the field of flow'ring grass;
    More gladsome to my withering joys that fade
    Than Winter's sun or Summer's cooling shade.

Sweeter than swelling grape of ripest wine,
Softer than feathers of the fairest swan ;
Smoother than jet, more stately than the pine,
Fresher than poplar, smaller than my span ;
    Clearer than Phœbus' fiery-pointed beam,
    Or icy crust of crystal's frozen stream.

Yet is she curster than the bear by kind,
And harder hearted than the agèd oak ;
More glib than oil, more fickle than the wind,
More stiff than steel, no sooner bent but broke :
    Lo ! thus my service is a lasting sore,
    Yet will I serve, although I die therefore.
                    Finis.   *Shep. Tony.*

THE SHEPHERD'S SORROW FOR HIS PHŒBE'S DISDAIN.

O WOODS ! unto your walks my body hies,
    To loose the traitorous bonds of tiring Love,
  Where trees, where herbs, where flowers,
    Their native moisture pours
From forth their tender stalks to help mine eyes :
Yet their united tears may nothing move.

When I behold the fair adornèd tree,
Which lightning's force and Winter's frost resists,
    Then Daphne's ill betide
    And Phœbus' lawless pride
Enforce me say, " Even such my sorrows be,
For self-disdain in Phœbe's heart consists."

If I behold the flowers by morning-tears,
Look lovely-sweet, ah ! then forlorn I cry,
 " Sweet showers for Memnon shed,
 All flowers by you are fed,
Whereas my piteous plaint that still appears,
Yields vigour to her scorns, and makes me die."

When I regard the pretty gleeful bird,
With tearful (yet delightful) notes complain,
 I yield a terror with my tears,
 And whilst her music wounds mine ears,
" Alas ! " say I, "when will my notes afford
Such like remorse, who still beweep my pain ? "

When I behold upon the leafless bough
The hapless bird lament her love's depart,
 I draw her biding nigh,
 And sitting down I sigh,
And sighing say, " Alas ! that birds avow
A settled faith, yet Phœbe scorns my smart."

Thus weary in my walk, and woful too,
I spend the day, forespent with daily grief;
 Each object of distress
 My sorrow doth express :
I dote on that which doth my heart undo,
And honour her that scorns to yield relief.
   Finis.   *I. F.*

ESPILUS AND THERION, THEIR CON-
TENTION IN SONG FOR THE
MAY-LADY.

Espilus.

TUNE up my voice, a higher note I yield ;
  To high conceit the song must needs be high :
More high than stars, more firm than flinty field,
Are all my thoughts, in which I live and die.
  Sweet soul, to whom I vowèd am a slave,
  Let not wild woods so great a treasure have.

Therion.

The highest note comes oft from basest mind,
As shallow brooks do yield the greatest sound ;
Seek other thoughts thy life or death to find,
Thy stars be fallen, plough'd is thy flinty ground :
  Sweet soul, let not a wretch that serveth sheep,
  Among his flocks so sweet a treasure keep.

Espilus.

Two thousand sheep I have, as white as milk,
Though not so white as is thy lovely face,
The pasture rich, the wool as soft as silk ;
All this I give, let me possess thy grace.
  But still take heed, lest thou thyself submit
  To one that hath no wealth, and wants his wit.

Therion.

Two thousand deer in wildest woods I have ;
Them can I take, but you I cannot hold :
He is not poor who can his freedom save ;
Bound but to you, no wealth but you I would.
But take this beast, if beasts you fear to miss,
For of his beasts the greatest beast he is.

Both kneeling to her Majesty.

Espilus.

Judge you, to whom all beauty's force is lent.

Therion.

Judge you of Love to whom all love is bent.

*This Song was sung before the Queen's most excellent
Majesty, in Wanstead Garden, as a contention between
a Forester and a Shepherd for the May-Lady.*
                    Finis. Sir Phil. Sidney.

OLD MELIBŒUS' SONG, COURTING
HIS NYMPH.

LOVE'S Queen, long waiting for her true-love,
        Slain by a boar which he had chased,
Left off her tears, and me embraced.
She kiss'd me sweet, and call'd me new Love ;
        With my silver hair she toy'd,
        In my stäid looks she joy'd.

"Boys," she said, "breed beauty's sorrow;
Old men cheer it even and morrow."
My face she named the seat of favour,
All my defects her tongue defended,
My shape she praised, but most commended
My breath, more sweet than balm in savour.
"Be, old man, with me delighted;
Love for love shall be requited."
With her toys at last she won me;
Now she coys that hath undone me.

THE SHEPHERD SYLVANUS HIS SONG.

MY life, young shepherdess, for thee
Of needs to death must post;
But yet my grief must stay with me
After my life is lost.

The grievous ill by death that cured is
Continually hath remedy at hand,
But not that torment that is like to this,
That in slow time and Fortune's means doth stand.

And if this sorrow cannot be
Ended with life (at most),
What then doth this thing profit me,
A sorrow won or lost?

Yet all is one to me, as now I try
A flattering hope, or that that had not been yet;
For if to-day for want of it I die,
Next day I do no less for having seen it.

Fain would I die to end and free
  This grief, that kills me most;
If that it might be lost with me,
  Or die when life is lost.
          Finis.   *Bar. Young.*

CORYDON'S SONG.

A BLITHE and bonny country lass,
  Heigho, bonny lass!
Sate sighing on the tender grass,
  And weeping said, "Will none come woo me?"
A smicker boy, a lither swain,
  Heigho, a smicker swain!
That in his love was wanton fain,
  With smiling looks straight came unto her.

Whenas the wanton wench espied,
  Heigho, when she espied!
The means to make herself a bride,
  She simper'd smooth like bonny-bell.
The swain that saw her squint-eyed kind,
  Heigho, squint-eyed kind!
His arms about her body twined,
  And said, "Fair lass, how fare ye, well?"

The country kit said, "Well forsooth,"
  Heigho, well forsooth!
"But that I have a longing tooth,
  A longing tooth that makes me cry."

"Alas!" said he, "what gars thy grief?"
　　Heigho, what gars thy grief?
"A wound," quoth she, "without relief:
　　I fear a maid that I shall die."

"If that be all," the shepherd said,
　　Heigho, the shepherd said!
"I'll make thee wive it, gentle maid,
　　And so recure thy malady."
Hereon they kiss'd with many an oath,
　　Heigho, many an oath!
And 'fore God Pan did plight their troth:
　　So to the church apace they hie.

And God send every pretty peat,
　　Heigho, the pretty peat!
That fears to die of this conceit,
　　So kind a friend to help at last.
Then maids shall never long again,
　　Heigho, to long again!
When they find ease for such a pain:
　　Thus my roundelay is past.
　　　　　　　　　Finis.　　　*Thom. Lodge.*

THE SHEPHERD'S SONNET.

MY fairest Ganymede, disdain me not,
　　Though silly shepherd I presume to love thee;
Though my harsh songs and sonnets cannot move
　　thee,
Yet to thy beauty is my love no blot:

Apollo, Jove, and many gods beside,
　'Sdain'd not the name of country shepherd swains,
　Nor want we pleasures, though we take some pains.
We live contentedly ; a thing call'd pride,
Which so corrupts the court and every place
　(Each place I mean where learning is neglected,
　And yet of late even learning's self's infected),
I know not what it means in any case.
　We only (when Molorchus 'gins to peep)
　Learn for to fold, and to unfold our sheep.

Finis.　　*Rich. Barnefield.*

SELVAGIA AND SYLVANUS, THEIR
SONGS TO DIANA.

Sel.　I SEE thee, jolly shepherd, merry,
　　　And firm thy faith, and sound as a berry.
Syl.　Love gave me joy, and fortune gave it,
　　　As my desire could wish to have it.

Sel.　What didst thou wish, tell me, sweet lover,
　　　Whereby thou might'st such joy recover ?
Syl.　To love where love should be inspirèd,
　　　Since there's no more to be desirèd.

Sel.　In this great glory and great gladness
　　　Think'st thou to have no touch of sadness ?
Syl.　Good fortune gave me not such glory,
　　　To mock my love, or make me sorry.

Sel. If my firm love I were denying,
  Tell me, with sighs wouldst thou be dying?
Syl. Those words (in jest) to hear thee speaking,
  For very grief this heart is breaking.

Sel. Yet wouldst thou change, I prithee tell me,
  In seeing one that did excel me?
Syl. O no! for how can I aspire
  To more than to mine own desire?

Sel. Such great affection dost thou bear me,
  As by thy words thou seem'st to swear me?
Syl. Of thy deserts, to which a debtor
  I am, thou mayst demand this better.

Sel. Sometimes methinks that I should swear it,
  Sometimes methinks thou shouldst not bear it.
Syl. Only in this my hap doth grieve me,
  And my desire, not to believe me.

Sel. Imagine that thou dost not love mine,
  But some brave beauty that's above mine.
Syl. To such a thing, sweet, do not will me,
  Where feigning of the same doth kill me.

Sel. I see thy firmness, gentle lover,
  More than my beauty can discover.
Syl. And my good fortune to be higher
  Than my desert, but not desire.
            Finis.   *Bar. Young.*

MONTANUS HIS MADRIGAL.

IT was a valley gaudy-green
  Where Dian at the fount was seen ;
        Green it was,
        And did pass
All other of Diana's bowers
In the pride of Flora's flowers.

A fount it was that no sun sees,
Circled in with cypress trees ;
        Set so nigh,
        As Phœbus' eye
Could not do the virgins scathe,
To see them naked when they bathe.

She sat there all in white,
Colour fitting her delight ;
        Virgins so.
        Ought to go,
For white in armoury is placed
To be the colour that is chaste.

Her taff'ta cassock you might see,
Tuckèd up above her knee,
        Which did show
        There below
Legs as white as whale's-bone ;
So white and chaste was never none.

L

Hard by her, upon the ground,
Sat her virgins in a round,
    Bathing their
    Golden hair,
And singing all in notes high :
" Fie on Venus' flattering eye !

" Fie on Love ! it is a toy,
Cupid witless and a boy,
    All his fires
    And desires
Are plagues that God sent from on high,
To pester men with misery."

As thus the virgins did disdain
Lovers' joy and lovers' pain,
    Cupid nigh
    Did espy,
Grieving at Diana's song,
Slily stole these maids among.

His bow of steel, darts of fire,
He shot amongst them sweet desire,
    Which straight flies
    In their eyes,
And at the entrance made them start,
For it ran from eye to heart.

Calisto straight supposèd Jove
Was fair and frolic for to love ;
    Dian she
    Scaped not free,
For, well I wot, hereupon
She loved the swain Endymion.

Clytie Phœbus, and Chloris' eye
Thought none so fair as Mercury ;
    Venus thus
    Did discuss
By her son in darts of fire,
None so chaste to check desire.

Dian rose with all her maids,
Blushing thus at Love's braids ;
    With sighs, all
    Show their thrall,
And flinging thence, pronounced this saw:
" What so strong as Love's sweet law ?"
        Finis.   *Ro. Greene.*

ASTROPHEL TO STELLA, HIS THIRD
SONG.

IF Orpheus' voice had force to breathe such music's
    love
Through pores of senseless trees, as it could make
    them move ;
If stones good measure danced, the Theban walls to
    build
To cadence of the tunes, which Amphion's lyre did
    yield ;
  More cause a like effect at leastwise bringeth ;
  O stones, O trees, learn hearing ! Stella singeth.

If Love might sweeten so a boy of shepherd's brood,
To make a lizard dull to taste Love's dainty food ;
If eagle fierce could so in Grecian maid delight,
As his light was her eyes, her death his endless night ;
    Earth gave that love ; heaven, I trow, Love
      refineth ;[1]
O beasts, O birds, look ! Love, lo ! Stella shineth.

The birds, stones and trees, feel this, and feeling, love ;
And if the trees nor stones stir not the same to prove,
Nor beasts nor birds do come unto this blessèd gaze,
Know, that small love is quick, and great love doth
    amaze.
    They are amazed, but you with reason armèd,
    O eyes, O ears of men, how are you charmèd ?

                 Finis.   *Sir. Phil. Sidney.*

A SONG BETWEEN SIRENUS AND

SYLVANUS.

Sirenus.

WHO hath of Cupid's cates and dainties preyèd
    May feed his stomach with them at his
    pleasure ;
If in his drink some ease he hath assayèd,
Then let him quench his thirsting without measure ;
    And if his weapons pleasant in their manner,
    Let him embrace his standard and his banner :
      For being free from him and quite exempted,
      Joyful I am, and proud, and well contented.

---

[1] *England's Helicon,* "defineth."

Sylvanus.

Of Cupid's dainty cates who hath not preyèd
May be deprivèd of them at his pleasure ;
If wormwood in his drink he hath assayèd,
Let him not quench his thirsting without measure ;
  And if his weapons in their cruel manner,
  Let him abjure his standard and his banner :
    For I not free from him, and not exempted,
    Joyful I am, and proud, and well contented.

Sirenus.

Love's so expert in giving many a trouble,
That now I know not why he should be praisèd ;
He is so false, so changing, and so double,
That with great reason he must be dispraisèd ;
  Love in the end is such a jarring passion,
  That none should trust unto his peevish fashion ;
    For of all mischief he's the only master,
    And to my good a torment and disaster.

Sylvanus.

Love's so expert in giving joy, not trouble,
That now I know not but he should be praisèd ;
He is so true, so constant, never double,
That in my mind he should not be dispraisèd ;
  Love in the end is such a pleasing passion,
  That every one may trust unto his fashion ;
    For of all good he is the only master,
    And foe unto my harms and my disaster.

Sirenus.

Not in these sayings to be proved a liar,
He knows that doth not love, nor is belovèd ;

Now nights and days I rest, as I desire,
After I had such grief from me removèd ;
  And cannot I be glad, since thus, estrangèd,
  Myself from false Diana I have changèd ?
    Hence, hence, false Love ! I will not entertain
      thee,
    Since to thy torments thou dost seek to train me.

Sylvanus.

Not in these sayings to be proved a liar,
He knows that loves, and is again belovèd ;
Now nights and days I rest in sweet desire,
After I had such happy fortune provèd ;
  And cannot I be glad, since not estrangèd,
  Myself into Selvagia I have changèd ?
    Come, come, good Love ! and I will entertain thee,
    Since to thy sweet content thou seek'st to train me.

Finis.   *Bar. Young.*

CERES' SONG IN EMULATION OF

CYNTHIA.

SWELL Ceres now, for other gods are shrinking !
  Pomona pineth,
    Fruitless her tree ;
    Fair Phœbus shineth
    Only on me.
Conceit doth make me smile whilst I am thinking
  How everyone doth read my story ;
  How every bough on Ceres low'reth,
  Cause heaven plenty on me poureth ;

And they in leaves do only glory,
All other gods of power bereaven,
Ceres only queen of heaven.

With robes and flowers let me be dressèd,
Cynthia that shineth
Is not so clear ;
Cynthia declineth
When I appear ;
Yet in this isle she reigns as blessed,
And everyone at her doth wonder ;
And in my ears still fond fame whispers,
" Cynthia shall be Ceres' mistress ; "
But first my car shall rive in sunder.
Help, Phœbus, help ! my fall is sudden ;
Cynthia, Cynthia ! must be sovereign !

*This Song was sung before her Majesty
at Bissam, the Lady Russell's, in progress. The Author's name unknown
to me.*

A PASTORAL ODE TO AN HONOURABLE

FRIEND.

AS to the blooming prime,
Bleak winter being fled,
From compass of the clime,
Where Nature lay as dead,
The rivers dull'd with time,
The green leaves witherèd,

Fresh Zephyri, the western brethren, be :
So th' honour of your favour is to me.

    For as the plains revive,
    And put on youthful green ;
    As plants begin to thrive,
    That disattired had been ;
    And arbours now alive,
    In former pomp are seen :
So if my Spring had any flowers before,
Your breath, Favonius, hath increased the store.

        Finis.   *E. B.*

A NYMPH'S DISDAIN OF LOVE.

" HEY, down, a down !" did Dian sing,
    Amongst her virgins sitting ;
" Than love there is no vainer thing,
    For maidens most unfitting."
And so think I, with a down, down, derry.

When women knew no woe,
    But lived themselves to please,
Men's feigning guiles they did not know,
    The ground of their disease.
Unborn was false suspect,
    No thought of jealousy ;
From wanton toys and fond affect,
    The virgin's life was free.
" Hey, down, a down !" did Dian sing, &c.

At length men usèd charms,
    To which what maids gave ear,
Embracing gladly endless harms,
    Anon enthrallèd were.
Thus women welcomed woe,
    Disguised in name of love,
A jealous hell, a painted show :
    So shall they find that prove.
" Hey, down, a down ! " did Dian sing,
    Amongst her virgins sitting ;
" Than love there is no vainer thing,
    For maidens most unfitting."
And so think I, with a down, down, derry.

        Finis.   *Ignoto.*

APOLLO'S LOVE SONG FOR FAIR
DAPHNE.

MY heart and tongue were twins at once
    conceived ;
The eldest was my heart, born dumb by destiny ;
The last my tongue, of all sweet thoughts bereaved,
Yet strung and tuned to play heart's harmony :
Both knit in one, and yet asunder placed.
What heart would speak, the tongue doth still discover ;
What tongue doth speak, is of the heart embraced :
And both are one, to make a new-found lover.
New-found, and only found in gods and kings,
Whose words are deeds, but deeds not words regarded.

Chaste thoughts do mount, and fly with swiftest wings,
My love with pain, my pain with loss rewarded.
    Engrave upon this tree Daphne's perfection :
    That neither men nor gods can force affection.

> *This Ditty was sung before her Majesty
> at the Right Honourable the Lord Chan-
> dos, at Sudley Castle, at her last being
> there in progress.   The Author thereof
> unknown.*

THE SHEPHERD DELICIUS HIS DITTY.

NEVER a greater foe did Love disdain,
        Or trod on grass so gay ;
Nor nymph green leaves with whiter hand hath rent ;
More golden hair the wind did never blow,
Nor fairer dame hath bound in white attire,
Or hath in lawn more gracious features tied,
    Than my sweet enemy.

Beauty and chastity one place refrain,
    In her bear equal sway,
Filling the world with wonder and content ;
But they do give me pain and double woe,
Since love and beauty kindled my desire,
And cruel chastity from me denied
    All sense of jollity.

There is no rose, nor lily after rain,
    Nor flower in month of May,

Nor pleasant mead, nor green in Summer sent,
That seeing them, my mind delighteth so,
As that fair flower which all the heavens admire,
Spending my thoughts on her, in whom abide
    All grace and gifts on high.

Methinks my heavenly nymph I see again
    Her neck and breast display,
Seeing the whitest ermine to frequent
Some plain, or flowers that make the fairest show.
O gods ! I never yet beheld her nigher,
Or far in shade, or sun, that satisfied
    I was in passing by.

The mead, the mount, the river, wood, and plain,
    With all their brave array,
Yield not such sweet as that fair face that's bent
Sorrows and joy in each soul to bestow
In equal parts, procured by amorous fire.
Beauty and Love in her their force have tried,
    To blind each human eye.

Each wicked mind and will, which wicked vice doth
    stain,
    Her virtues break and stay ;
All airs infect by air are purged and spent,
Though of a great foundation they did grow.
O body, that so brave a soul dost hire !
And blessed soul, whose virtues ever pried
    Above the starry sky !

Only for her my life in joys I train,
    My soul sings many a lay ;
Musing on her, new seas I do invent

Of sovereign joy, wherein with pride I row.
The deserts for her sake I do require,
For without her the springs of joy are dried,
 And that I do defy.

Sweet fate, that to a noble deed dost strain
 And lift my heart to-day,
Sealing her there with glorious ornament !
Sweet seal, sweet grief, and sweetest overthrow !
Sweet miracle, whose fame cannot expire !
Sweet wound, and golden shaft, that so espied
 Such heavenly company
 Of beauty's graces in sweet virtues dyed,
As like were never in such years descried !
    Finis.   *Bar. Young.*

AMYNTAS FOR HIS PHYLLIS.

AURORA now began to rise again
 From watery couch and from old Tithon's side,
In hope to kiss upon Actæan plain
Young Cephalus ; and through the golden glide
On eastern coast [s]he cast so great a light,
That Phœbus thought it time to make retire
From Thetis' bower, wherein he spent the night,
To light the world again with heavenly fire.

No sooner gan his wingèd steeds to chase
The Stygian night, mantled with dusky veil,
But poor Amyntas hasteth him apace,
In deserts thus to weep a woful tale :

"You silent shades, and all that dwell therein,
As birds, or beasts, or worms that creep on ground,
Dispose yourselves to tears, while I begin
To rue the grief of miné eternal wound.

"And doleful ghosts where Nature flies the light,
Come seat yourselves with me on every side;
And while I die for want of my delight,
Lament the woes through fancy me betide.
Phyllis is dead, the mark of my desire,
My cause of love, and shipwreck of my joys;
Phyllis is gone, that set my heart on fire,
That clad my thoughts with ruinous annoys.

"Phyllis is fled, and bides I wot not where,
Phyllis, alas! the praise of womankind;
Phyllis, the sun of this our hemisphere,
Whose beams made me and many others blind;
But blinded me, poor swain, above the rest,
That like old Œdipus I live in thrall;
Still feel the worst, and never hope the best,
My mirth in moan, and honey drown'd in gall.

"Her fair but cruel eyes bewitch'd my sight,
Her sweet but fading speech enthrall'd my thought,
And in her deeds I reapèd such delight
As brought both will and liberty to hought.
Therefore all hope of happiness, adieu!
Adieu, desire, the source of all my care!
Despair tells me my weal will ne'er renew,
Till thus my soul doth pass in Charon's crare.

" Meantime my mind must suffer Fortune's scorn,
My thoughts still wound, like wounds that still are
    green,
My weaken'd limbs be laid on beds of thorn ;
My life decays, although my death's foreseen.
Mine eyes, now eyes no more, but seas of tears,
Weep on your fill, to cool my burning breast,
Where Love did place desire, 'twixt hope and fears ;
I say desire, the author of unrest.

" And would to God, Phyllis ! where'er thou be,
Thy soul did see the sour of mine estate ;
My joys eclipsed for only want of thee,
My being with myself at foul debate ;
My humble vows, my sufferance of woe,
My sobs, and sighs, and ever-watching eyes ;
My plaintive tears, my wand'ring to and fro,
My will to die, my never-ceasing cries.

" No doubt but then these sorrows would persuade
The doom of death to cut my vital twist,
That I with thee amidst th' infernal shade,
And thou with me might sport us as we list.
Oh, if thou wait on fair Proserpine's train,
And hearest Orpheus near the Elysian springs,
Entreat thy queen to free thee thence again,
And let the Thracian guide thee with his strings ! "
             Finis.   *Tho. Watson.*

FAUSTUS AND FIRMIUS SING TO THEIR NYMPH BY TURNS.

Firmius. OF mine own self I do complain,
   And not for loving thee so much,
   But that indeed thy power is such,
 That my true love it doth restrain,
 And only this doth give me pain ;
   For fain I would
   Love her more, if that I could.

Faustus. Thou dost observe who doth not see,
   To be beloved a great deal more ;
   And yet thou shalt not find such store
 Of love in others as in me ;
 For all I have I give to thee,
   Yet fain I would
   Love thee more, if that I could.

Firmius. O try no other shepherd swain,
   And care not other loves to prove ;
   Who though they give thee all their love,
 Thou canst not such as mine obtain ;
 And wouldst thou have in love more gain ?
   O yet I would
   Love thee more, if that I could.

Faustus. Impossible it is, my friend,
   That anyone should me excel
   In love, whose love I will refell,

> If that with me he will contend ;
> My love no equal hath, nor end.
> And yet I would
> Love her more, if that I could.

Firmius. Behold ! how love my soul hath charm'd !
> Since first thy beauties I did see
> (Which is but little yet to me),
> My freest senses I have harm'd
> (To love thee), leaving them unarm'd ;
> And yet I would
> Love thee more, if that I could.

Faustus. I ever gave and give thee still
> Such store of love as Love hath lent me ;
> And therefore well thou mayst content
>   thee,
> That Love doth so enrich my fill ;
> But now behold my chiefest will,
> That fain I would
> Love thee more, if that I could.
>   *Finis.*   *Bar. Young.*

SIRENO, A SHEPHERD,

HAVING A LOCK OF HIS FAIR NYMPH'S HAIR WRAPT ABOUT WITH GREEN SILK, MOURNS THUS IN A LOVE-DITTY.

WHAT changes here, O hair,
  I see since I saw you !
How ill fits you this green to wear,
For hope the colour due !

Indeed, I well did hope,
Though hope were mix'd with fear,
No other shepherd should have scope
Once to approach this heare.[1]

Ah, hair ! how many days
My Dian made me show,
With thousand pretty childish plays,
If I ware you or no !
Alas ! how oft with tears,
(Oh, tears of guileful breast !)
She seemèd full of jealous fears,
Whereat I did but jest !

Tell me, O hair of gold,
If I then faulty be,
That trust those killing eyes I would,
Since they did warrant me ?
Have you not seen her mood,
What streams of tears she spent,
Till that I sware my faith so stood,
As her words had it bent ?

Who hath such beauty seen,
In one that changeth so ?
Or where one's[2] love so constant been,
Who ever saw such woe ?
Ah, hairs, are you[3] not grieved,
To come from whence you be,
Seeing how once you saw I lived,
To see me as you see ?

[1] I have kept this eccentric spelling ("heare ' for "hair")
for the sake of the rhyme.
[2] So 1598 *Astrophel and Stella* (appended to *Arcadia*).
England's Helicon "one loves."
[3] So ed. 1598. *E. H.* "you are."

M

On sandy bank of late,
I saw this woman sit,
Where, *Sooner die than change my state,*
She with her finger writ.
Thus my belief was stay'd
(Behold Love's mighty hand)
On things were by a woman said
And written in the sand !

> *Translated by Sir Phil. Sidney, out*
> *of Diana of Montmaior.*

A SONG BETWEEN TAURISIUS AND DIANA,

ANSWERING VERSE FOR VERSE.

Taurisius. THE cause why that thou dost deny
   To look on me, sweet foe, impart ?

Diana. Because that doth not please the eye
   Which doth offend and grieve the heart.

Taurisius. What woman is, or ever was,
   That when she looketh, could be moved?

Diana. She that resolves her life to pass,
   Neither to love nor to be loved.

Taurisius. There is no heart so fierce and hard,
   That can so much torment a soul.

Diana. Nor shepherd of so small regard,
   That reason will so much control.

-Taurisius. How falls it out love doth not kill
   Thy cruelty with some remorse?

Diana.   Because that love is but a will,
            And free-will doth admit no force.
Taurisius. Behold, what reason now thou hast
            To remedy my loving smart !
Diana.   The very same binds me as fast,
            To keep such danger from my heart.
Taurisius. Why dost thou thus torment my mind,
            And to what end thy beauty keep ?
Diana.   Because thou call'st me still unkind,
            And pitiless when thou dost weep.
Taurisius. Is it because thy cruelty
            In killing me doth never end ?
Diana.   Nay, for because I mean thereby,
            My heart from sorrow to defend.
Taurisius. Be bold ; so foul I am no way
            As thou dost think, fair shepherdess.
Diana.   With this content thee, that I say
            That I believe the same no less.
Taurisius. What, after giving me such store
            Of passions, dost thou mock me too ?
Diana.   If answers thou wilt any more,
            Go seek them without more ado.

                    Finis.   *Bar. Young.*

ANOTHER SONG BEFORE HER MAJESTY
AT OXFORD,

SUNG BY A COMELY SHEPHERD, ATTENDED ON BY
SUNDRY OTHER SHEPHERDS AND NYMPHS.

HERBS, words, and stones, all maladies have
  cured ;
 Herbs, words, and stones, I usèd when I loved ;
Herbs smells, words wind, stones hardness have
  procured :
 By stones, nor words, nor herbs her mind was
  moved.
I ask'd the cause ; this was a woman's reason :—
 'Mongst herbs are weeds, and thereby are refused ;
Deceit as well as truth speaks words in season ;
 False stones by foils have many one abused.
I sigh'd, and then she said my fancy smoked ;
 I gazed, she said my looks were follies glancing ;
I sounded dead, she said my love was choked ;
 I started up, she said, my thoughts were dancing.
  Oh, sacred Love ! if thou have any godhead,
  Teach other rules to win a maidenhead.
     Finis.   *Anonymous.*

THE SHEPHERD'S SONG: A CAROL OR HYMN FOR CHRISTMAS.

S WEET Music, sweeter far
    Than any song is sweet ;
Sweet Music, heavenly rare,
    Mine ears (O peers !) doth greet.
You gentle flocks, whose fleeces, pearl'd with dew,
Resemble heaven, whom golden drops make bright,
Listen, O listen ! now, O not to you
Our pipes make sport to shorten weary night.
    But voices most divine,
    Make blissful harmony ;
    Voices that seem to shine,
    For what else clears the sky ?
Tunes can we hear, but not the singers see ;
The tunes divine, and so the singers be.

    Lo ! how the firmament
    Within an azure fold
    The flock of stars hath pent,
    That we might them behold.
Yet from their beams proceedeth not this light,
Nor can their crystals such reflection give.
What, then, doth make the element so bright ?
The heavens are come down upon earth to live.
    But hearken to the song :
    "Glory to glory's King !
    And peace all men among !"
    These choristers do sing.
Angels they are, as also, shepherds, he
Whom in our fear we do admire to see.

"Let not amazement blind
Your souls," said he, "annoy;
To you and all mankind,
My message bringeth joy.
For, lo ! the world's great Shepherd now is born,
A blessed babe, an infant full of power ;
After long night uprisen is the morn,
Renowning Bethlem in the Saviour.
    Sprung is the perfect day,
    By prophets seen afar ;
    Sprung is the mirthful May,
    Which Winter cannot mar."
In David's city doth this sun appear,
Clouded in flesh, yet, shepherds, sit we here?

Finis.   *E. B.*

ARSILIUS HIS CAROL FOR JOY OF THE NEW MARRIAGE BETWEEN SIRENUS AND DIANA.

LET now each mead with flowers be depainted,
    Of sundry colours, sweetest odours glowing ;
Roses yield forth your smells so finely tainted,
    Calm winds the green leaves move with gentle
        blowing.
    The crystal rivers flowing
    With waters be increased ;
    And since each one from sorrow now hath ceased,
    From mournful plaints and sadness,
    Ring forth, fair nymphs, your joyful songs for
        gladness !

Let springs and meads all kind of sorrow banish,
    And mournful hearts the tears that they are bleeding ;
Let gloomy clouds with shining morning vanish,
    Let every bird rejoice that now is breeding.
        And since, by new proceeding,
        With marriage now obtained,
        A great content by great contempt is gained,
        And you devoid of sadness,—
        Ring forth, fair nymphs, your joyful songs for
            gladness !

Who can make us to change our firm desires,
    And soul to leave her strong determination,
And make us freeze in ice, and melt in fires,
    And nicest hearts to love with emulation ?
        Who rids us from vexation,
        And all our minds commandeth,
        But great Felicia, that his might withstandeth,
        That fill'd our hearts with sadness ?
        Ring forth, fair nymphs, your joyful songs for
            gladness !

Your fields with their distilling favours cumber,
    Bridegroom and happy bride, each heavenly power !
Your flocks, with double lambs increased in number,
    May never taste unsavoury grass and sour !
        The Winter's frost and shower
        Your kids, your pretty pleasure,
        May never hurt ! and blest with so much treasure,
        To drive away all sadness,
        Ring forth, fair nymphs, your joyful songs for
            gladness !

Of that sweet joy delight you with such measure,
　Between you both fair issue to engender ;
Longer than Nestor may you live in pleasure ;
　　The gods to you such sweet content surrender,
　　　That may make mild and tender
　　　The beasts in every mountain,
　　　And glad the fields and woods and every fountain,
　　　Abjuring former sadness.
　　　Ring forth, fair nymphs, your joyful songs for
　　　　gladness !

Let amorous birds with sweetest notes delight you,
　Let gentle winds refresh you with their blowing ;
Let fields and forests with their good requite you,
　　And Flora deck the ground where you are going,
　　　Roses and violets strowing,
　　　The jasmine and the gilliflower,
　　　With many more, and never in your bower
　　　To taste of household sadness.
　　　Ring forth, fair nymphs, your joyful songs for
　　　　gladness !

Concord and peace hold you for aye contented,
　And in your joyful state live you so quiet,
That with the plague of jealousy tormented
　　You may not be, nor fed with fortune's diet,
　　　And that your names may fly yet
　　　To hills unknown with glory.
　　　But now because my breast, so hoarse and sorry
　　　It faints, may rest from singing,
　　　End, nymphs, your songs, that in the clouds are
　　　　ringing.

　　　　　　　Finis.　　　*Bar. Young.*

PHILISTUS' FAREWELL TO FALSE CLORINDA.

CLORINDA false, adieu ! thy love torments me.
 Let Thyrsis have thy heart, since he contents thee.
Oh, grief and bitter anguish !
 For thee I languish ;
Fain I, alas ! would hide it,
 Oh ! but who can abide it ?
I[1] cannot I, abide it.
Adieu, adieu then,
 Farewell !
Leave my death now desiring,
For thou hast thy requiring.
Thus spake Philistus on his hook relying,
 And sweetly fell a-dying.
     Finis. *Out of M. Morley's*
         Madrigals.

ROSALIND'S MADRIGAL.

LOVE in my bosom like a bee,
 Doth suck his sweet ;
Now with his wings he plays with me,
 Now with his feet.
Within mine eyes he makes his nest,
His bed amidst my tender breast ; ·

[1] So the song-book. *England's Helicon* " I can I cannot I."

My kisses are his daily feast,
And yet he robs me of my rest.
    Ah, wanton, will ye?

And if I sleep, then percheth[1] he,
    With pretty slight,[2]
And makes his pillow of my knee,
    The livelong night.
Strike I my lute, he tunes the string ;
He music plays if I but sing ;[3]
He lends me every lovely thing ;
Yet cruel he my heart doth sting.
    Whist, wanton, still ye !

Else I with roses every day
    Will whip ye hence,
And bind ye, when ye long to play,
    For your offence.
I'll shut my eyes to keep ye in,
I'll make you fast it for your sin,
I'll count your power not worth a pin.
Alas ! what hereby shall I win
    If he gainsay me?

What if I beat the wanton boy
    With many a rod ?
He will repay me with annoy,
    Because a god.

---

[1] This is the reading in Lodge's *Rosalind*, 1590. *England's Helicon* "pierceth."

[2] In Lodge's *Rosalind* the reading is " flight."

[3] *Rosalind* reads " if so I sing."

Then sit thou safely on my knee,
And let thy bower my bosom be ;
Lurk in mine eyes, I like of thee.
O Cupid ! so thou pity me,
 Spare not, but play thee.
   Finis.   *Thom. Lodge.*

A DIALOGUE SONG BETWEEN SYLVANUS
AND ARSILIUS.

Syl.   SHEPHERD, why dost thou hold thy peace ?
    Sing, and thy joy to us report.
Arsil.   My joy, good shepherd, should be less,
    If it were told in any sort.
Syl.   Though such great favours thou dost win,
    Yet deign thereof to tell some part.
Arsil.   The hardest thing is to begin
    In enterprises of such art.
Syl.   Come, make an end, no cause omit,
    Of all the joys that thou art in.
Arsil.   How should I make an end of it,
    That am not able to begin ?
Syl.   It is not just we should consent
    That thou shouldst not thy joys recite.
Arsil.   The soul that felt the punishment,
    Doth only feel this great delight.
Syl.   That joy is small, and nothing fine,
    That is not told abroad to many.
Arsil.   If it be such a joy as mine,
    It never can be told to any.

Syl.   How can this heart of thine contain
    A joy that is of such great force ?
Arsil.   I have it, where I did retain
    My passions of.so great remorse.
Syl.   So great and rare a joy is this,
    No man is able to withhold.
Arsil.   But greater that a pleasure is,
    The less it may with words be told.
Syl.   Yet have I heard thee heretofore,
    Thy joys in open songs report.
Arsil.   I said, I had of joy some store,
    But not how much, nor in what sort.
Syl.   Yet when a joy is in excess,
    Itself it will oft-times unfold.
Arsil.   Nay, such a joy would be the less,
    If but a word thereof were told.
                Finis.   *Bar. Young.*

MONTANUS' SONNET.

WHEN the dog,
    Full of rage,
With his ireful eyes
Frowns amidst the skies,
The shepherd to assuage
The fury of the heat,
Himself doth safely seat
    By a fount
    Full of fair,
Where a gentle breath,
Mounting from beneath,

Tempereth the air.
There his flocks
Drink their fill
And with ease repose,
While sweet sleep doth close
Eyes from toiling ill ;
But I burn,
Without rest ;
No defensive power
Shields from Phœbus' lower,
Sorrow is my best.
Gentle Love !
Lower no more ;
If thou wilt invade
In the secret shade,
Labour not so sore ;
I myself,
And my flocks,
They their love to please,
I myself to ease,
Both leave the shady oaks,
Content to burn in fire
Sith Love doth so desire.
Finis.   *S. E. D.*

THE NYMPH SELVAGIA HER SONG.

SHEPHERD, who can pass such wrong,
And a life in woes so deep,
Which to live is too-too long,
As it is too short to weep?

Grievous sighs in vain I waste,
　　Leesing my affiance, and
I perceive my hope at last,
　　With a candle in the hand.

What time then to hope among
　　Bitter hopes that never sleep?
When this life is too-too long,
　　As it is too short to weep.

This grief which I feel so rife,
　　Wretch, I do deserve as hire;
Since I came to put my life
　　In the hands of my desire.

Then cease not my complaints so strong;
　　For, though life her course doth keep,
It is not to live so long,
　　As it is too short to weep.
　　　　　　　Finis.　　　　*Bar. Young.*

THE HERDMAN'S HAPPY LIFE.

WHAT pleasure have great princes
　　More dainty to their choice
Than herdmen wild, who careless
　　In quiet life rejoice?
And fortune's fate not fearing,
Sing sweet in summer morning.

Their dealings plain and rightful,
    Are void of all deceit ;
They never know how spiteful
    It is to kneel and wait
On favourite presumptuous,
Whose pride is vain and sumptuous.

All day their flocks each tendeth,
    At night they take their rest,
More quiet than who sendeth
    His ship into the east,
Where gold and pearl are plenty,
But getting very dainty.

For lawyers and their pleading,
    They 'steem it not a straw ;
They think that honest meaning,
    Is of itself a law ;
Where conscience judgeth plainly,
They spend no money vainly.

Oh, happy who thus liveth !
    Not caring much for gold ;
With clothing which sufficeth,
    To keep him from the cold.
Though poor and plain his diet,
Yet merry it is and quiet.

        Finis.   *Out of M. Bird's*
                      Set Songs.

CYNTHIA THE NYMPH HER SONG TO
FAIR POLYDORA.

NEAR to the river banks, with green
　　And pleasant trees on every side,
Where freest minds would most have been,
That never felt brave Cupid's pride,
　　To pass the day and tedious hours
　　Amongst those painted meads and flowers,

A certain shepherd, full of woe,
Sirenus call'd, his flocks did feed,
Not sorrowful in outward show,
But troubled with such grief indeed,
　　As cruel love is wont t'impart
　　Unto a painful loving heart.

This shepherd every day did die,
For love he to Diana bare ;
A shepherdess so fine perdie,
So lively, young, and passing fair,
　　Excelling more in beauty's feature,
　　Than any other human creature.

Who had not any thing of all
She had, but was extreme in her ;
For meanly wise none might her call,
Nor meanly fair, for he did err
　　If so he did ; but should devise
　　Her name of passing fair and wise.

Favours on him she did bestow,
Which if she had not, then be sure
He might have suffered all that woe,
Which afterward he did endure,
   When he was gone, with lesser pain,
   And at his coming home again.

For when indeed the heart is free
From suffering pain or torment's smart,
If wisdom does not oversee,
And beareth not the greatest part,
   The smallest grief and care of mind
   Doth make it captive to their kind.

Near to a river swift and great,
That famous Ezla had to name,
The careful shepherd did repeat
The fears he had by absence blame,
   Which he suspect where he did keep,
   And feed his gentle lambs and sheep.

And now sometimes he did behold
His shepherdess, that thereabout
Was on the mountains of that old
And ancient Leon seeking out
   From place to place the pastures best
   Her lambs to feed, herself to rest.

And sometime musing, as he lay,
When on those hills she was not seen,
Was thinking of that happy day,
When Cupid gave him such a queen
   Of beauty, and such cause of joy,
   Wherein his mind he did employ.

N

Yet said, poor man, when he did see
Himself so sunk in sorrow's pit,
The good that Love hath given me,
I only do imagine it,
　Because this nearest harm and trouble;
　Hereafter I should suffer double.

The sun for that it did decline,
The careless man did not offend
With fiery beams, which scarce did shine
But that which did of love depend,
　And in his heart did kindle fire
　Of greater flames and hot desire.

Him did his passions all invite;
The green leaves blown with gentle wind,
Crystalline streams with their delight,
And nightingales were not behind,
　To help him in his loving verse,
　Which to himself he did rehearse.
　　　　　　Finis.　　　*Bar. Young.*

THE SHEPHERD TO THE FLOWERS.

SWEET violets, Love's paradise, that spread
　Your gracious odours, which you couchèd bear
Within your paly faces,
Upon the gentle wing of some calm breathing wind,
　That plays amidst the plain,
　If by the favour of propitious stars you gain

Such grace as in my lady's bosom place to find,
  Be proud to touch those places,
And when her warmth your moisture forth doth wear,
Whereby her dainty parts are sweetly fed,
    Your honours of the flowery meads I pray,
    You pretty daughters of the earth and sun,
    With mild and seemly breathing straight display
    My bitter sighs, that have my heart undone.

Vermilion roses, that with new day's rise
Display your crimson folds fresh-looking, fair,
  Whose radiant bright disgraces
The rich adornèd rays of roseate rising morn.
    Ah ! if her virgin's hand
    Do pluck your pure, ere Phœbus view the land,
And veil your gracious pomp in lovely Nature's scorn ;
    If chance my mistress traces
Fast by your flowers to take the Summer's air,
Then, woful blushing, tempt her glorious eyes,
    To spread their tears, Adonis' death reporting,
    And tell Love's torments,[1] sorrowing for her friend,
    Whose drops of blood within your leaves consorting,
    Report fair Venus' moans to have no end.
Then may remorse, in pitying of my smart.
Dry up my tears, and dwell within her heart.
           Finis.   *Ignoto.*

[1] Ed. 1614, " torment."

THE SHEPHERD ARSILIUS HIS SONG
TO · HIS REBECK.

NOW love and fortune turn to me again,
     And now each one enforceth and assures
A hope, that was dismayèd, dead, and vain;
And from the harbour of mishaps recures [1]
     A heart that is consumed in burning fire,
     With unexpected gladness, that adjures [2]
My soul to lay aside her mourning tire,
     And senses to prepare a place for joy;
     Care in oblivion endless shall expire;
For every grief of that extreme annoy,
     Which, when my torment reign'd, my soul, alas!
     Did feel, the which long absence did destroy,
Fortune so well appays, that never was
     So great the torment of my passèd ill,
     As is the joy of this same good I pass.
Return, my heart, sursaulted with the fill ·
     Of thousand great unrests and thousand fears;
     Enjoy thy good estate, if that thou will.
And wearied eyes, leave off your burning tears,
     For soon you shall behold her with delight,
     For whom my spoils with glory Cupid bears.
Senses which seek my star so clear and bright,
     By making here and there your thoughts estray,
     Tell me, what will you feel before her sight?

[1] This is the reading found in Young's *Diana*, 1598, p. 136
(whence the poem is taken). *England's Helicon* " assures."
[2] So *Diana*. *E. H.* " admires."

Hence solitariness, torments away,
  Felt for her sake ! and wearied members cast
  Off all your pain, redeem'd this happy day !
Oh, stay not, Time, but pass with speedy haste,
  And Fortune hinder not her coming now !
  O God ! betides me yet this grief at last ?
Come, my sweet shepherdess, the life which thou,
  Perhaps, didst think was ended long ago,
  At thy command is ready still to bow.
Comes not my shepherdess desirèd so ?
  O God ! what if she's lost, or if she stray
  Within this wood, where trees so thick do grow ?
Or if this nymph that lately went away,
  Perhaps forgot to go and seek her out ?
  No, no, in her oblivion never lay.
Thou only art my shepherdess, about
  Whose thoughts my soul shall find her joy and rest ;
  Why com'st not then to assure it from doubt ?
Oh, seest thou not the sun pass to the west ?
  And if it pass and I behold thee not,
  Then I my wonted torments will request,
  And thou shalt wail my hard and heavy lot.
                    Finis.   *Bar. Young.*

ANOTHER OF ASTROPHEL TO HIS
STELLA.

IN a grove most rich of shade,
  Where birds wanton music made,
May, then young, his pied weeds showing,
New perfumed, with flowers fresh growing,

Astrophel with Stella sweet
Did for mutual comfort meet,
Both within themselves oppress'd,
But each in the other bless'd.

Him great harms had taught much care,
Her fair neck a foul yoke bare ;
But her sight his cares did banish,
In his sight her yoke did vanish.
Wept they had, alas ! the while,
But now tears themselves did smile,
While their eyes, by love directed,
Interchangeably reflected.

Sigh they did, but now betwixt
Sighs of woe were glad sighs mix'd ;
With arms cross'd, yet testifying
Restless rest, and living dying.
Their ears hungry of each word
Which the dear tongue would afford,
But their tongues restrain'd from walking,
Till their hearts had ended talking.

But when their tongues could not speak,
Love itself did silence break ;
Love did set his lips asunder,
Thus to speak in love and wonder :
"Stella, sovereign of my joy,
Fair triumpher of annoy !
Stella, star of heavenly fire !
Stella, loadstar of desire !

"Stella, in whose shining eyes,
Are the lights of Cupid's skies,
Whose beams where they once are darted,
Love therewith is straight imparted !
Stella, whose voice when it speaks,

Senses all asunder breaks !
Stella, whose voice when it singeth,
Angels to acquaintance bringeth !
   " Stella, in whose body is
Writ each character of bliss,
Whose face all, all beauty passeth,
Save thy mind, which it surpasseth ;
Grant, O grant ! but speech, alas !
Fails me, fearing on to pass ;
Grant—O me, what am I saying?
But no fault there is in praying.
   " Grant, O dear ! on knees I pray,"
(Knees on ground he then did stay,)
" That[1] not I, but since I love you,
Time and place for me may move you.
Never season was more fit,
Never room more apt for it.
Smiling air allows my reason ;
The[se] birds sing, now use the season.
   " This small wind, which so sweet is,
See how it the leaves doth kiss !
Each tree in his best attiring,
Sense of love to love inspiring.
Love makes earth the water drink ;
Love to earth makes water sink.
And if dumb things be so witty,
Shall a heavenly grace want pity ?"
   There his hands, in their speech, fain,
Would have made tongue's language plain,

---

1 Eds. 1591 of *Astrophel and Stella* read :
     " That not I, but since I proue you,
     Time and place from me nere moue you."

But her hands his hands repelling,[1]
Gave repulse, all grace excelling.
Then[2] she spake; her speech was such,
As not ears, but heart did touch;
While such wise she love denied,
As yet love she signified.

　"Astrophel," said she, "my love
Cease in these effects to prove.
Now be still, yet still believe me,
Thy grief more than death doth grieve me.
If that any thought in me
Can taste comfort but of thee,
Let me feed with hellish anguish, .
Joyless, helpless, endless languish.

　"If those eyes you praisèd be
Half so dear as you to me,
Let me home return stark blinded
Of those eyes, and blinder minded.
If to secret of my heart
I do any wish impart
Where thou art not foremost placed,
Be both wish and I defaced.

　"If more may be said, I say,
All my bliss on thee I lay.
If thou love, my love content thee,
For all love, all faith is meant thee.
Trust me, while I thee deny,
In myself the smart I try.

---

[1] Eds. 1591 of *Astrophel and Stella* give "compelling" in
this line and "expelling" in the next.
[2] The lines "Then she spake . . . . I should blush when
thou art named" were added in the 1598 *Astrophel and Stella*
(appended to *Arcadia*).

Tyrant honour doth thus use thee,
Stella's self might not refuse thee.
" Therefore, dear, this no more move,
Lest, though I leave not thy love,
Which too deep in me is framed,
I should blush when thou art named."
Therewithal away she went,
Leaving him to passion rent,
With what she had done and spoken,
That therewith my song is broken.

Finis.   *Sir Phil. Sidney.*

SIRENUS HIS SONG TO DIANA'S FLOCKS.

PASSED contents,
   Oh, what mean ye?
Forsake me now, and do not weary me.
Wilt thou hear me, O memory?
My pleasant days, and nights again,
I have appay'd with sevenfold pain.
Thou hast no more to ask me why,
For when I went they all did die,
   As thou dost see ;
   Oh ! leave me then, and do not weary me.

Green field and shadow'd valley, where
Sometime my chiefest pleasure was,
Behold what I did after pass.
Then let me rest, and if I bear
Not with good cause continual fear,
   Now do you see,
   Oh ! leave me then, and do not trouble me.

I saw a heart changèd of late,
And wearied to assure mine ;
Then I was forced to recure mine
By good occasion, time and fate ;
My thoughts that now such passion hate,
    Oh ! what mean ye ?
    Forsake me now and do not weary me.

You lambs and sheep that in these lays
Did sometime follow me so glad ;
The merry hours and the sad
Are passèd now, with all those days.
Make not such mirth and wonted plays
    As once did ye ;
    For now no more, you have deceivèd me.

If that to trouble me you come,
Or come to comfort me indeed ;
I have no ill for comfort's need.
But if to kill me ; then (in sum),
Now my joys are dead and dumb,
    Full well may ye
    Kill me, and you shall make an end of me.
          Finis.   *Bar. Young.*

TO AMARYLLIS.

THOUGH Amaryllis dance in green,
    Like fairy queen,
    And sing full clear
    With smiling cheer ;
Yet since her eyes make heart so sore,
Heigho ! chill love no more.

My sheep are lost for want of food,
    And I so wood,
    That all the day
I sit and watch a herdmaid gay,
Who laughs to see me sigh so sore ;
Heigho ! chill love no more.

Her loving looks, her beauty bright,
    Is such delight,
    That all in vain
I love to like and lose my gain,
For her that thanks me not therefore ;
Heigho ! chill love no more.

Ah, wanton eyes ! my friendly foes
    And cause of woes,
    Your sweet desire
Breeds flames of ice and freeze in fire.
You scorn to see me weep so sore ;
Heigho ! chill love no more.

Love ye who list, I force him not ;
    Sith God it wot
    The more I wail,
The less my sighs and tears prevail.
What shall I do ? but say therefore,
Heigho ! chill love no more.

        Finis.   *Out of M. Bird's*
                       Set Songs.

CARDENIA THE NYMPH TO HER FALSE
SHEPHERD FAUSTUS.

FAUSTUS, if thou wilt read from me
    These few and simple lines,
By them most clearly thou shalt see
How little should accounted be
    Thy feignèd words and signs.
For noting well thy deeds unkind,
    Shepherd, thou must not scan,
That ever it came to my mind,
To praise thy faith like to the wind,
    Or for a constant man.

For this in thee shall so be found,
    As smoke blown in the air ;
Or like quicksilver turning round ;
Or as a house built on the ground
    Of sands that do impair.
To firmness thou art contrary,
    More slipp'ry than the eel ;
Changing as weathercock on high,
Or the chameleon on the dye,
    Or fortune's turning wheel.

Who would believe thou wert so free,
    To blaze me thus each hour ?
My shepherdess, thou liv'st in me,
My soul doth only dwell in thee,
    And every vital power ;

Pale Atropos my vital string
    Shall cut, and life offend ;
The stream shall first turn to their spring ;
The world shall end, and everything,
    Before my love shall end.

This love that thou didst promise me,
    Shepherd, where is it found ?
The word and faith I had of thee,
Oh, tell me now where may they be,
    Or where may they resound ?
Too soon thou didst the title gain
    Of giver of vain words ;
Too soon my love thou didst obtain,
Too soon thou lov'dst Diana in vain,
    That nought but scorn affords.

But one thing now I will thee tell,
    That much thy patience moves ;
That though Diana doth excel
In beauty, yet she keeps not well
    Her faith, nor loyal proves ;
Then thou hast chosen, each one saith,
    Thine equal, and a shrow ;
For if thou hast undone thy faith,
Her love and lover she betrayeth :
    So like to like may go.

If now this sonnet, which I send,
    Will anger thee, before
Remember, Faustus (yet my friend),
That if these speeches do offend,
    Thy deeds do hurt me more.

Then let each one of us amend ;
   Thou deeds, I words so spent ;
For I confess I blame my pen,
Do thou as much, so in the end
   Thy deeds thou do repent.
            Finis.   *Bar. Young.*

OF PHYLLIDA.

A S I beheld I saw a herdman wild .
   With his sheep-hook a picture fine deface,
Which he sometime, his fancy to beguile,
   Had carved on bark of beech in secret place ;
And with despite of most afflicted mind,
   Through deep despair of heart, for love dismay'd,
He pull'd even from the tree the carvèd rind,
   And, weeping sore, these woful words he said :
" Ah, Phyllida, would God thy picture fair
   I could as lightly blot out of my breast !
Then should I not thus rage in deep despair,
   And tear the thing sometime I likèd best.
     But all in vain ! it booteth not, God wot,
     What printed is in heart, on tree to blot."
           Finis.   *Out of M. Bird's*
                     Set Songs.

MELISEA HER SONG IN SCORN OF HER SHEPHERD NARCISSUS.

YOUNG shepherd, turn aside, and move
   Me not to follow thee ;
For I will neither kill with love,
   Nor love shall not kill me.

Since I will live and never [1] favour show,
   Then die not, for my love I will not give.
For I will never have thee love me so,
   As I do mean to hate thee while I live.

That since the lover so doth prove
   His death, as thou dost see,
Be bold, I will not kill with love,
   Nor love shall not kill me.
        Finis.   *Bar. Young.*

HIS ANSWER TO THE NYMPH'S SONG.

IF to be loved it thee offend,
   I cannot choose but love thee still ;
And so thy grief shall have no end,
   Whiles that my life maintains my will.

[1] So Young's *Diana*, 1598. *England's Helicon* omits the word "favour."

Oh I let me yet with grief complain,
  Since such a torment I endure ;
Or else fulfil thy great disdain,
  To end my life with death most sure.
For as no credit thou wilt lend,
  And as my love offends thee still,
So shall thy sorrows have no end,
  Whiles that my life maintains my will.

If that by knowing thee I could
  Leave off to love thee as I do ;
Not to offend thee, then I would
  Leave off to like and love thee too.
But since all love to thee doth tend,
  And I of force must love thee still,
Thy grief shall never have an end,
  Whiles that my life maintains my will.
                    Finis.   *Bar. Young.*

HER PRESENT ANSWER AGAIN TO HIM.

METHINKS thou tak'st the worser way,
  Enamour'd shepherd, and in vain,
That thou wilt seek thine own decay,
  To love her that doth thee disdain.

For thine own self, thy woful heart
  Keep still, else art thou much to blame ;
For she to whom thou gav'st each part
  Of it disdains to take the same.

Follow not her that makes a play
 And jest of all thy grief and pains ;
And seek not, shepherd, thy decay,
 To love her that thy love disdains.
                         Finis.   *Bar. Young.*

HIS LAST REPLY.

SINCE thou to me wert so unkind,
  Myself I never loved, for
I could not love him in my mind,
  Whom thou, fair mistress, dost abhor.

If viewing thee, I saw thee not,
  And seeing thee, I could not love thee ;
Dying, I should not live, God wot,
  Nor living should to anger move thee.

But it is well that I do find
  My life so full of torments, for
All kind of ills do fit his mind,
  Whom thou, fair mistress, dost abhor.

In thy oblivion buried now,
  My death I have before mine eyes ;
And here to hate myself I vow,
  As cruel thou dost me despise.

Contented ever thou didst find
  Me with thy scorns, though never (for
To say the truth) I joy'd in mind,
  After thou didst my love abhor.
                 Finis.   *Bar. Young.*

O

PHILON THE SHEPHERD HIS SONG.

WHILE that the sun with his beams hot
  Scorchèd the fruits in vale and mountain,
Philon, the shepherd, late forgot,
Sitting beside a crystal fountain
  In shadow of a green oak tree,
  Upon his pipe this song play'd he :
" Adieu love, adieu love, untrue love !
Untrue love, untrue love, adieu love !
Your mind is light, soon lost for new love.

" So long as I was in your sight,
I was [1] your heart, your soul, and treasure ;
And evermore you sobb'd and sigh'd,
Burning in flames beyond all measure.
  Three days endured your love to me,
  And it was lost in other three.
Adieu love, adieu love, untrue love ! &c.

" Another shepherd you did see,
To whom your heart was soon enchainèd ;
Full soon your love was leapt from me,
Full soon my place he had obtainèd ;
  Soon came a third, your love to win,
  And we were out, and he was in.
Adieu love, &c.

   [1] Ed. 1600 " I was as."

"Sure you have made me passing glad,
That you your mind so soon removèd,
Before that I the leisure had,
To choose you for my best belovèd ;
   For all your love was past and done,
   Two days before it was begun.
Adieu love, &c."

       Finis.   *Out of M. Bird's
              Set Songs.*

LYCORIS THE NYMPH HER SAD SONG.

IN dew of roses steeping
   Her lovely cheeks,[1]
Lycoris thus sat weeping :
"Ah, Dorus false, that hast my heart bereft me,
And now unkind hast left me,
   Hear, alas ! oh, hear me !
    Ay me, ay me,
   Cannot my beauty move thee ?
   . Pity, yet pity me,
  'Because I love thee.
Ay me, thou scorn'st the more I pray thee ;
And this thou dost, and all to slay me.
Why,[2] do then kill me, and vaunt thee ;
Yet my ghost still shall haunt thee."

       Finis.   *Out of M. Morley's
              Madrigals.*

[1] In *England's Helicon* the words "Her lovely cheeks" are printed as part of the first line.
[2] *England's Helicon* divides this line and the next, thus :—
      "Why do then
    Kill me, and vaunt thee :
      Yet my ghost
    Still shall haunt thee."

TO HIS FLOCKS.

BURST forth, my tears, assist my forward grief,
  And show what pain imperious love provokes !
Kind tender lambs, lament love's scant relief,
And pine, since pensive care my freedom yokes.
  Oh, pine to see me pine, my tender flocks !

Sad pining care, that never may have peace,
At beauty's gate in hope of pity knocks ;
But mercy sleeps, while deep disdains increase,
And beauty hope in her fair bosom locks.[1]
  Oh, grieve to hear my grief, my tender flocks !

Like to the winds my sighs have wingèd been,
Yet are my sighs and suits repaid with mocks ;
I plead, yet she repineth at my teen.
Oh, ruthless rigour, harder than the rocks,
  That both the shepherd kills, and his poor flocks !
                    Finis.

TO HIS LOVE.

COME away ! come, sweet love !
  The golden morning breaks ;
All the earth, all the air,
Of love and pleasure speaks.

[1] The old editions give "yoakes."

Teach thine arms then to embrace,
And sweet rosy lips to kiss,
And mix our souls in mutual bliss.
Eyes were made for beauty's grace,
Viewing, rueing, love's long pain,
Procured by beauty's rude disdain.

Come away! come, sweet love!
The golden morning wastes,
While the sun from his sphere
His fiery arrows casts,
Making all the shadows fly,
Playing, staying in the grove,
To entertain the stealth of love.
Thither, sweet love, let us hie
Flying, dying, in desire,
Wing'd with sweet hopes and heavenly fire.

Come away! come, sweet love!
Do not in vain adorn [1]
Beauty's grace that should rise
Like to the naked morn.
Lilies on the river's side,
And fair Cyprian flowers new-blown,
Desire no beauties but their own;
Ornament is nurse of pride.
Pleasure, measure love's delight.
Haste then, sweet love, our wishèd flight!
Finis.

[1] Old eds. "adiorne."

ANOTHER OF HIS CYNTHIA.

A WAY with these self-loving lads,
  Whom Cupid's arrow never glads !
Away poor souls that sigh and weep,
In love of them that lie and sleep !
    For Cupid is a meadow god,
    And forceth none to kiss the rod.

God Cupid's shaft, like destiny,
Doth either good or ill decree ;
Desert is borne out of his bow,
Reward upon his feet doth go :
    What fools are they that have not known
    That Love likes no laws but his own !

My songs they be of Cynthia's praise,
I wear her rings on holidays ;
On every tree I write her name,
And every day I read the same :
    Where Honour Cupid's rival is,
    There miracles are seen of his.

If Cynthia crave her ring of me,
I blot her name out of the tree ;
If doubt do darken things held dear,
Then " Welfare nothing !" once a year :
    For many run, but one must win,
    Fools only hedge the cuckoo in.

The worth that worthiness should move,
Is love, which is the due of Love ;
And love as well the shepherd[1] can, -
As can the mighty nobleman :
   Sweet nymph, 'tis true, you worthy be,
   Yet without love nought worth to me.
Finis.

ANOTHER TO HIS CYNTHIA.

MY Thoughts are wing'd with Hopes, my Hopes
     with Love ;
Mount Love unto the moon in clearest night,
And say, as she doth in the heavens move,
On earth so wanes and waxeth my delight :
   And whisper this, but softly, in her ears,
   " Hope oft doth hang the head and Trust shed tears.

And you, my Thoughts, that some mistrust do carry,
If for mistrust my mistress do you blame,
Say, though you alter, yet you do not vary,
As she doth change and yet remain the same :
   Distrust doth enter hearts, but not infect,
   And Love is sweetest season'd with Suspect.

If she for this with clouds do mask her eyes,
And make the heavens dark with her disdain,

1 " Foster " (=forester) is the reading in the Song-book.

With windy sighs disperse them in the skies,
Or with thy tears dissolve them into rain,
   Thoughts, Hopes, and Love, return to me no more,
   Till Cynthia shine as she hath done before. .
        Finis.

*These three ditties were taken out of Master
John Dowland's Book of Tableture for the
Lute. The Authors' names not there set
down, and therefore left to their owners.*

MONTANUS' SONNET IN THE WOODS.

ALAS, how wander I amidst these woods,
   Whereas no day-bright shine doth find access !
But where the melancholy fleeting floods,
Dark as the night, my night of woes express,
Disarm'd of reason, spoil'd of Nature's goods,
Without redress to salve my heaviness
  I walk, whilst thought, too cruel to my harms,
 · With endless grief my heedless judgment charms.

My silent tongue assail'd by secret fear,
My traitorous eyes imprison'd in their joy ;
My fatal peace devour'd in feignèd cheer,
My heart enforced to harbour in annoy ; ·
My reason robb'd of power by yielding care,
My fond opinions slave to every joy.
  O Love ! thou guide in my uncertain way,
  Woe to thy bow, thy fire, the cause of my decay !
        Finis.   *S. E. D.*

THE SHEPHERD'S SORROW, BEING
DISDAINED IN LOVE.

MUSES, help me! sorrow swarmeth,
　Eyes are fraught with seas of languish;
Hapless hope my solace harmeth,
Mind's repast is bitter anguish.

Eye of day regarded never,
Certain trust in world untrusty;
Flattering hope beguileth ever,
Weary old, and wanton lusty.

Dawn of day beholds enthronèd
Fortune's darling proud and dreadless;
Darksome night doth hear him moanèd,
Who before was rich and needless.

Rob the sphere of lines united,
Make a sudden void in nature;
Force the day to be benighted,
Reave the cause of time and creature.

Ere the world will cease to vary,
This I weep for, this I sorrow;
Muses, if you please to tarry,
Further help I mean to borrow.

Courted once by fortune's favour,
Compass'd now with envy's curses;
All my thoughts of sorrows savour,
Hopes run fleeting like the sources.

Ay me ! wanton scorn hath maimèd
All the joys my heart enjoyèd ;
Thoughts their thinking have disclaimèd,
Hate my hopes have quite annoyèd.

Scant regard my weal hath scanted,
Looking coy hath forced my low'ring ;
Nothing liked, where nothing wanted,
Weds mine eyes to ceaseless show'ring.

Former love was once admirèd,
Present favour is estrangèd ;
Loathed the pleasure long desirèd,
Thus both men and thoughts are changèd.

Lovely swain, with lucky speeding,
Once, but now no more so friended ;
You my flocks have had in feeding,
From the morn till day was ended.

Drink and fodder, food and folding,
Had my lambs and ewes together ;
I with them was still beholding,
Both in warmth and winter weather.

Now they languish, since refusèd,
Ewes and lambs are pain'd with pining ;
I with ewes and lambs confusèd,
All unto our deaths declining.

Silence, leave thy cave obscurèd,
Deign a doleful swain to tender ;
Though disdains I have endurèd,
Yet I am no deep offender.

Philip's son can with his finger
Hide his scar, it is so little ;
Little sin a day to linger,
Wise men wander in a tittle.

Trifles yet my swain have turnèd,
Though my sun he never showeth ;
Though I weep, I am not mournèd ;
Though I want, no pity groweth.

Yet for pity, love my Muses,
Gentle Silence be their cover ;
They must leave their wonted uses,
Since I leave to be a lover.

They shall live with thee enclosèd,
I will loathe my pen and paper ;
Art shall never be supposèd,
Sloth shall quench the watching taper.

Kiss them, Silence ! kiss them kindly,
Though I leave them, yet I love them ;
Though my wit have led them blindly,
Yet a swain did once approve them.

I will travel soils removèd,
Night and morning never merry ;
Thou shalt harbour that I lovèd,
I will love that makes me weary.

If perchance the shepherd strayeth
In thy walks and shades unhaunted ;
Tell the teen my heart betrayeth,
How neglect my joys have daunted.

Finis.   *Thom. Lodge.*

A PASTORAL SONG BETWEEN PHYLLIS
AND AMARYLLIS,

TWO NYMPHS, EACH ANSWERING OTHER

LINE FOR LINE.

FIE on the sleights that men devise,
    Heigho, silly sleights !
When simple maids they would entice,
    Maids are young men's chief delights.
Nay, women they witch with their eyes,
    Eyes like beams of burning sun,
And men once caught, they soon despise,
    So are shepherds oft undone.

If any young man win a maid,
    Happy man is he ;
By trusting him she is betray'd,
    Fie upon such treachery !
If maids win young men with their guiles,
    Heigho, guileful grief !
They deal like weeping crocodiles,
    That murder men without relief.

I know a simple country hind,
    Heigho, silly swain !
To whom fair Daphne proved kind :
    Was he not kind to her again ?
He vow'd by Pan with many an oath,
    Heigho, shepherd's god is he !
Yet since hath changed and broke his troth,
    Troth-plight broke will plaguèd be.

She had deceivèd many a swain,
  Fie on false deceit !
And plighted troth to them in vain,
  There can be no grief more great.
Her measure was with measure paid,
  Heigho, heigho, equal meed !
She was beguiled that had betray'd,
  So shall all deceivers speed.

If every maid were like to me,
  Heigho, hard of heart !
Both love and lovers scorn'd should be,
  Scorners shall be sure of smart.
If every maid were of my mind,
  Heigho, heigho, lovely sweet !
They to their lovers should prove kind,
  Kindness is for maidens meet.

Methinks, love is an idle toy,
  Heigho, busy pain !
Both wit and sense it doth annoy,
  Both sense and wit thereby we gain.
Tush, Phyllis, cease ! be not so coy,
  Heigho, heigho, coy disdain !
I know you love a shepherd's boy,
  Fie that maidens so should feign.

Well, Amaryllis, now I yield,
  Shepherds, pipe aloud !
Love conquers both in town and field,
  Like a tyrant fierce and proud.

The evening star is up ye see,
    Vesper shines, we must away ;
Would every lover might agree !
So we end our roundelay.
            Finis.   *H. C.*

THE SHEPHERD'S ANTHEM.

NEAR to a bank with roses set about,
    Where pretty turtles joining bill to bill,
And gentle springs steal softly murmuring out,
Washing the foot of pleasure's sacred hill,
    There little Love sore wounded lies,
        His bow and arrows broken,
    Bedew'd with tears from Venus' eyes ;
        Oh, that it should be spoken !

Bear him my heart, slain with her scornful eye,
Where sticks the arrow that poor hart did kill,
With whose sharp pile, yet will him ere he die,
About my heart to write his latest will.
    And bid him send it back to me,
        At instant of his dying,
    That cruel, cruel she may see,
        My faith and her denying.

His hearse shall be a mournful cypress shade,
And for a chantry Philomel's sweet lay ;
Where prayer shall continually be made
By pilgrim lovers passing by that way,

With nymphs' and shepherds' yearly moan,
   His timeless death beweeping;
And telling that my heart alone
   Hath his last will in keeping.
               Finis.   *Mich. Drayton.*

THE COUNTESS OF PEMBROKE'S
PASTORAL.

A SHEPHERD and a shepherdess
   Sat keeping sheep upon the downs;
His looks did gentle blood express,
   Her beauty was no food for clowns;
   Sweet lovely twain, what might you be?

Two fronting hills bedeck'd with flowers,
   They chose to be each other's seat,
And there they stole their amorous hours
   With sighs and tears, poor lovers' meat;
   Fond Love! thou feed'st thy servants so.

"Fair friend," quoth he, "when shall I live,
   That am half dead, yet cannot die?
Can beauty such sharp guerdon give,
   To him whose life hangs in your eye?"
   Beauty is mild and will not kill.

"Sweet swain," quoth she, "accuse not me,
   That long have been thy humble thrall;
But blame the angry destiny,
   Whose kind consent might finish all."
   Ungentle fate, to cross true love!

Quoth he, " Let not our parents' hate,
　Disjoin what Heaven hath link'd in one.
They may repent and all too late,
　If childless they be left alone."
　Father nor friend should wrong true love.

"The parent's frown," said she, " is death,
　To children that are held in awe ;
From them we drew our vital breath,
　They challenge duty then by law."
　Such duty as kills not true love.

" They have," quoth he, "a kind of sway
　On these our earthly bodies here ;
But with our souls deal not they may,
　The god of love doth hold them dear."
　He is most meet to rule true love.

" I know," said she, " 'tis worse than hell,
　When parent's choice must please our eyes ;
Great hurt comes thereby, I can tell;
　Forced love in desperate danger dies."
　Fair maid, then fancy thy true love.

" If we," quoth he, "might see the hour
　Of that sweet state which never ends,
Our heavenly gree might have the power,
　To make our parents as dear friends."
　All rancour yields to sovereign love.

"Then god of love," she said, "consent,
　And show some wonder of thy power ;
Our parents and our own content
　May be confirm'd by such an hour."
　Grant, greatest god ! to further love.

The fathers, who did always tend,
   When thus they got their private walk,
As happy fortune chanced to send,
  · Unknown to each, heard all this talk ;
   Poor souls to be so cross'd in love !

Behind the hills whereon they sat,
   They lay this while and listen'd all,
And were so movèd both thereat,
   That hate in each began to fall ;
   Such is the power of sacred love.

They show'd themselves in open sight ;
   Poor lovers, Lord, how they were mazed !
And hand in hand the fathers plight,
   Whereat, poor hearts ! they gladly gazed ;
   Hope now begins to further love.

And to confirm a mutual band
   Of love, that at no time should cease,
They likewise joinèd hand in hand
   The shepherd and the shepherdess ;
   Like fortune still befall true love !
         Finis.   *Shep. Tony.*

ANOTHER OF ASTROPHEL.

THE nightingale, so soon as April bringeth
   Unto her rested sense a perfect waking,
While late-bare earth, proud of new clothing springeth,
Sings out her woes, a thorn her song-book making ;

P

And, mournfully bewailing,
Her throat in tunes expresseth,
What grief her breast oppresseth,
For Tereus' force on her chaste will prevailing.
Oh, Philomela fair! oh, take some gladness
That here is juster cause of plaintful sadness!
Thine earth now springs, mine fadeth;
Thy thorn [1] without, my thorn my heart invadeth!

Alas! she hath no other cause of languish
But Tereus' love, on her by strong hand wroken;
Wherein she suffering all her spirits languish,
Full woman-like complains her will was broken.
    But I, who daily craving,
    Cannot have to content me,
    Have more cause to lament me,
    Sith wanting is more woe than too much having.
Oh, Philomela fair! oh, take some gladness
That here is juster cause of plaintful sadness!
Thine earth now springs, mine fadeth;
Thy thorn without, my thorn my heart invadeth!
                Finis.   Sir Phil. Sidney.

AN [2] INVECTIVE AGAINST LOVE.

ALL is not gold that shineth bright in show;
    Not every flower so good as fair to sight;
The deepest streams above do calmest·flow,
And strongest poisons oft the taste delight.
    The pleasant bait doth hide the harmful hook,
    And false deceit can lend a friendly look.

1 Ed. 1614 "throne."
2 This poem was added in ed. 1614.

Love is the gold whose outward hue doth pass,
Whose first beginnings goodly promise make
Of pleasures fair and fresh as summer's grass,
Which neither sun can parch nor wind can shake ;
   But when the mould should in the fire be tried,
   The gold is gone, the dross doth still abide.

Beauty the flower so fresh, so fair, so gay,
So sweet to smell, so soft to touch and taste,
As seems it should endure, by right, for aye,
And never be with any storm defaced ;
   But when the baleful southern wind doth blow,
   Gone is the glory which it erst did show.

Love is the stream whose waves so calmly flow,
As might entice men's minds to wade therein ;
Love is the poison mix'd with sugar so,
As might by outward sweetness liking win ;
   But as the deep o'erflowing stops thy breath,
   So poison once received brings certain death.

Love is the bait whose taste the fish deceives,
And makes them swallow down the choking hook ;
Love is the face whose fairness judgment reaves,
And makes thee trust a false and feignèd look ;
   But as the hook the foolish fish doth kill,
   So flattering looks the lover's life doth spill.
              Finis.

FAIR PHYLLIS AND HER SHEPHERD.

"SHEPHERD, saw you not
  My fair lovely Phyllis
Walking on this mountain,
  Or on yonder plain?
She is gone this way to Diana's fountain,
  And hath left me wounded,
   With her high disdain.
 Ay me, she is fair,
 And without compare!
   Sorrow, come and sit with me;
  Love is full of fears,
  Love is full of tears,
   Love without these cannot be.
Thus my passions pain me,
For my Love hath slain me;
   Gentle shepherd, bear a part;
Pray to Cupid's mother,
For I know no other
   That can help to ease my smart."

"Shepherd, I have seen
  Thy fair, lovely Phyllis,
Where her flocks are feeding,
  By the river's side;
Oh! I much admire
  She, so far exceeding
In surpassing beauty,
  Should surpass in pride.

But, alas! I find,
They are all unkind;
    Beauty knows her power too well.
  When they list they love,
  When they please they move,   `
    Thus they turn our heaven to hell.
For their fair eyes glancing,
Like to Cupid's dancing,
    Roll about still to deceive us;
With vain hopes deluding,
Still dispraise concluding,
    Now they love, and now they leave us."

" Thus I do despair,
    Have her I shall never;
If she be so coy,
    Lost is all my love;
But she is so fair
    I must love her ever;
All my pain is joy,
    Which for her I prove.
If I should her try,
And she should deny,
    Heavy heart with woe will break.
  Though against my will,
  Tongue thou must be still,
    For she will not hear thee speak.
Then with sighs go prove her,
Let them show I love her;
    Gracious Venus, be my guide!
But though I complain me,
She will still disdain me;
    Beauty is so full of pride."

"What though she be fair?
 Speak, and fear not speeding ;
Be she ne'er so coy,
 Yet she may be won ;
Unto her repair,
 Where her flocks are feeding,
Sit and tick and toy,
 Till set be the sun.
 Sun then being set,
 Fear not Vulcan's net,
  Though that Mars therein was caught ;
 If she do deny,
 Thus to her reply,
  Venus' laws she must be taught.
Then with kisses move her,
That's the way to prove her,
  Thus thy Phyllis must be won ;
She will not forsake thee,
But her Love will make thee,
  When Love's duty once is done."

"Happy shall I be,
 If she grant me favour,
Else for love I die ;
 Phyllis is so fair."
"Boldly then go see,
 Thou mayst quickly have her ;
Though she should deny
 Yet do not despair."
 "She is full of pride ;
 Venus be my guide !
 Help a silly shepherd's speed !"
 "Use no such delay,

Shepherd, go thy way,
    Venture, man, and do the deed."
" I will sore complain me."
" Say that Love hath slain thee
    If her favours do not feed ;
But take no denial,
Stand upon thy trial ;
    Spare to speak, and want of speed."
        Finis.   *I. G.*

THE SHEPHERD'S SONG OF VENUS
AND ADONIS.

VENUS fair did ride,
    Silver doves they drew her,
By the pleasant lawnds
    Ere the sun did rise ;
Vesta's beauty rich
    Open'd wide to view her,
Philomel records
    Pleasing harmonies.
Every bird of spring
Cheerfully did sing,
    Paphos' goddess they salute ;
Now Love's queen so fair,
Had of mirth no care,
    For her son had made her mute.
In her breast so tender
He a shaft did enter,
    When her eyes beheld a boy ;

Adonis was he namèd,
By his mother shamèd,
  Yet he now is Venus' joy.

Him alone she met,
  Ready bound for hunting,
Him she kindly greets,
  And his journey stays ;
Him she seeks to kiss
  No devices wanting,
Him her eyes still woo,
  Him her tongue still prays.
He with blushing red
Hangeth down the head,
  Not a kiss can he afford ;
His face is turn'd away,
Silence said her nay,
  Still she woo'd him for a word.
"Speak," she said, " thou fairest,
Beauty thou impairest ;
  See me, I am pale and wan.
Lovers all adore me,
I for love implore thee ; "
  Crystal tears with that down ran.

Him herewith she forced
  To come sit down by her,
She his neck embraced,
  Gazing in his face ;
He like one transform'd,
  Stirr'd no look to eye her,
Every herb did woo him
  Growing in that place.

Each bird with a ditty,
Prayèd him for pity
   In behalf of Beauty's queen ;
Waters' gentle murmur
Cravèd him to love her,
   Yet no liking could be seen.
" Boy," she said, " look on me ;
Still I gaze upon thee ;
   Speak, I pray thee, my delight !"
Coldly he replièd,
And in brief denièd
   To bestow on her a sight.

" I am now too young
   To be won by beauty,
Tender are my years,
   I am yet a bud."
" Fair thou art," she said,
   " Then it is thy duty,
Wert thou but a blossom,
   To effect my good.
Every beauteous flower
Boasteth in my power,
   Birds and beasts my laws effect ;
Myrrha, thy fair mother,
Most of any other
   Did my lovely hests respect.
Be with me delighted,
Thou shalt be requited,
   Every nymph on thee shall tend ;
All the gods shall love thee,
Man shall not reprove thee,
   Love himself shall be thy friend."

" Wend thee from me, Venus ;
   I am not disposèd ;
Thou wring'st me too hard ;
   Prithee, let me go.
Fie, what a pain it is
   Thus to be enclosèd !
If love begin with labour,
   It will end in woe."
" Kiss me, I will leave."
" Here a kiss receive."
   " A short kiss I do it find.
Wilt thou leave me so ?
Yet thou shalt not go.
   Breathe once more thy balmy wind ;
It smelleth of the myrrh-tree,
That to the world did bring thee ;
   Never was perfume so sweet."
When she had thus spoken,
She gave him a token,
   And their naked bosoms meet.

" Now," he said, " let's go.
   Hark, the hounds are crying !
Grisly boar is up ;
   Huntsmen follow fast."
At the name of boar,
   Venus seemèd dying,
Deadly-coloured pale,
   Roses overcast.
" Speak," said she, " no more
Of following the boar,
   Thou, unfit for such a chase.
Course the fearful hare,

Venison do not spare.
  If thou wilt yield Venus grace,
Shun the boar, I pray thee,
Else I still will stay thee."
  Herein he vow'd to please her mind.
Then her arms enlargèd,
Loth she him dischargèd ;
  Forth he went as swift as wind.

Thetis Phœbus' steeds
  In the west retainèd,
Hunting-sport was past,
  Love her Love did seek.
Sight of him too soon,
  Gentle queen, she gainèd ;
On the ground he lay,
  Blood had left his cheek.
For an orpèd swine
Smit him in the groin ;
  Deadly wound his death did bring.
Which when Venus found,
She fell in a swound,
  And, awaked, her hands did wring.
Nymphs and satyrs skipping,
Came together tripping,
  Echo every cry express'd ;
Venus by her power
Turn'd him to a flower,
  Which she weareth in her crest.
            Finis.   *H. C.*

THYRSIS THE SHEPHERD HIS
DEATH'S SONG.

THYRSIS to die desirèd,
    Marking her eyes that to his heart was nearest ;
And she that with his flame no less was firèd,
    Said to him, "Oh, heart's love ! dearest !
      Alas, forbear to die now !
      By thee I live, by thee I wish to die too !"

Thyrsis[1] that heat refrainèd,
    Wherewith to die, poor lover, then he hasted,
Thinking it death while he his looks maintainèd
    Full fixèd on her eyes, full of pleasure,
    And lovely nectar sweet from them he tasted.
His dainty nymph, that now at hand espièd
      The harvest of love's treasure,
    Said thus, with eyes all trembling, faint and wasted,
      "I die now !"
    The shepherd then replièd,
      "And I, sweet life, do die too !"

[1] In the song-book the stanza runs thus :—

    "Thyrsis that heat refrainèd
      Wherewith in haste to die he did betake him,
    Thinking it death that life would not forsake him,
      And while his look full fixèd he retainèd,
      On her eyes full of pleasure,
    And lovely nectar sweet" &c.

Thus these two lovers fortunately dièd,
   Of death so sweet, so happy, and so desirèd,
   That to die so again their life retirèd.
              Finis.   *Out of Master M. Young's*
                         Musica Transalpina.

ANOTHER STANZA ADDED AFTER.

THYRSIS enjoy'd the graces
   Of Chloris' sweet embraces,
Yet both their joys were scanted,
   For dark it was and candlelight they wanted.
Wherewith kind Cynthia in the heaven that shinèd
   Her nightly veil resignèd,
   And her fair face disclosèd
Where Love and Joy were met and both reposèd :[1]
   Then each from other's looks such joy derivèd,
   That both with mere delight died and revivèd.
              Finis.   *Out of the same.*

ANOTHER SONNET THENCE TAKEN.

ZEPHYRUS brings the time that sweetly scenteth
   With flowers and herbs which winter's frost
      exileth ;
Progne now chirpeth, Philomel lamenteth,
   Flora the garlands white and red compileth ;

---

[1] This line is omitted in *England's Helicon ;* it is found in the
song-book.

Fields do rejoice, the frowning sky relenteth,
　Jove to behold his dearest daughter smileth ;
The air, the water, the earth to joy consenteth,
　Each creature now to love him reconcileth.
But with me, wretch, the storms of woe perséver,
　And heavy sighs which from my heart she straineth,
That took the key thereof to heaven for ever ;
　So that singing of birds and springtime's flow'ring,
And ladies' love that men's affection gaineth,
　Are like a desert and cruel beasts devouring.
　　　　　　Finis.

THE SHEPHERD'S SLUMBER.

IN peascod time, when hound to horn
　Gives ear till buck be kill'd,
And little lads with pipes of corn
　Sat keeping beasts a-field,
I went to gather strawberries tho,
　By woods and groves full fair ;
And parch'd my face with Phœbus so,
　In walking in the air,
That down I laid me by a stream,
　With boughs all over-clad ;
And there I met the strangest dream
　That ever shepherd had.
Methought I saw each Christmas game,
　Each revel all and some,
And everything that I can name,
　Or may in fancy come.

The substance of the sights I saw
   In silence pass they shall,
Because I lack the skill to draw
   The order of them all ;
But Venus shall not pass my pen,
   Whose maidens in disdain
Did feed upon the hearts of men
   That Cupid's bow had slain.
And that blind boy was all in blood,
   Be-bath'd up[1] to the ears,
And like a conqueror he stood,
   And scornèd lover's tears.
"I have," quoth he, "more hearts at call
   Than Cæsar could command,
And like the deer I make them fall,
   That runneth o'er the lawnd.
One drops down here, another there ;
   In bushes as they groan,
I bend a scornful careless ear,
   To hear them make their moan."
" Ah, sir," quoth Honest Meaning then,
   " Thy boy-like brags I hear ;
When thou hast wounded many a man,
   As huntsman doth the deer,
Becomes it thee to triumph so ?
   Thy mother wills it not ;
For she had rather break thy bow,
   Than thou should'st play the sot."
" What saucy merchant speaketh now ? "
   Said Venus in her rage ;
" Art thou so blind thou know'st not how
   I govern every age ?

[1] Ed. 1600 omits the word "up."

My son doth shoot no shaft in waste,
  To me the boy is bound ;
He never found a heart so chaste,
  But he had power to wound."
" Not so, fair goddess," quoth Free-will,
  " In me there is a choice ;
And cause I am of mine own ill
  If I in thee rejoice.
And when I yield myself a slave
  To thee, or to thy son,
Such recompense I ought not have,
  If things be rightly done."
" Why, fool," stepp'd forth Delight and said,
  " When thou art conquer'd thus,
Then, lo ! dame Lust, that wanton maid,
  Thy mistress is, I wus.
And Lust is Cupid's darling dear,
  Behold her where she goes ;
She creeps the milk-warm flesh so near,
  She hides her under close,
Where many privy thoughts do dwell,
  A heaven here on earth ;
For they have never mind of hell,
  They think so much on mirth."
" Be still, Good Meaning," quoth Good Sport,
  " Let Cupid triumph make ;
For sure his kingdom shall be short,
  If we no pleasure take.
Fair Beauty, and her play-pheers gay,
  The virgins vestal too,
Shall sit and with their fingers play,
  As idle people do.
If Honest Meaning fall to frown,

And I Good Sport decay,
Then Venus' glory will come down
　And they will pine away."
"Indeed," quoth Wit, "this your device
　With strangeness must be wrought;
And where you see these women nice,
　And looking to be sought,
With scowling brows their follies check,
　And so give them the fig;
Let Fancy be no more at beck,
　When Beauty looks so big."
When Venus heard how they conspired
　To murther women so,
Methought indeed the house was fired,
　With storms and lightning tho.
The thunderbolt through windows burst,
　And in their steps a wight,
Which seem'd some soul or sprite accurst,
　So ugly was the sight.
"I charge you, ladies all," quoth he,
　"Look to yourselves in haste;
For if that men so wilful be,
　And have their thoughts so chaste,
That[1] they can tread on Cupid's breast,
　And march on Venus' face,
Then they shall sleep in quiet rest,
　When you shall wail your case!"
With that had Venus all in spite
　Stirr'd up the dames to ire;
And Lust fell cold, and Beauty white
　Sat babbling with Desire,

---

[1] So ed. 1614.—Ed. 1600, "And they can," &c.

Whose mutt'ring words I might not mark,
  Much whispering there arose;
The day did lower, the sun wax'd dark,
  Away each lady goes.
But whither went this angry flock?
  Our Lord himself doth know.
Wherewith full loudly crew the cock,
  And I awakèd so.
A dream, quoth I, a dog it is,
  I take thereon no keep;
I gage my head such toys as this
  Doth spring from lack of sleep.

Finis.   *Ignoto.*

DISPRAISE[1] OF LOVE AND LOVERS'
FOLLIES.

IF love be life, I long to die,
  Live they that list for me;
And he that gains the most thereby,
  A fool at least shall be;
But he that feels the sorest fits,
'Scapes with no less than loss of wits.
    Unhappy life they gain
    Which love do entertain!

In day by feignèd looks they live,
  By lying dreams in night,

---

1 This poem was added in ed. 1614.

Each frown a deadly wound doth give,
  Each smile a false delight.
If't hap their lady pleasant seem,
It is for other's love they deem ;
    If void she seem of joy,
    Disdain doth make her coy.

Such is the peace that lovers find,
  Such is the life they lead,
Blown here and there with every wind,
  Like flowers in the mead ;
Now war, now peace, now war again,
Desire, despair, delight, disdain ;
    Though dead, in midst of life ;
    In peace, and yet at strife.

        Finis.   *Ignoto.*

ANOTHER SONNET.

IN wonted walks since wonted fancies change,
  Some cause there is, which of strange cause doth
    rise,
For in each thing whereto my mind doth range
Part of my pain meseems engravèd lies.

The rocks which were of constant mind, the mark
In climbing steep, now hard refusal show ;
The shading woods seem now my sun to dark,
And stately hills disdain to look so low.

The restful caves now restless visions give ;
In dales I see each way a hard ascent ;
Like late-mown meads, late cut from joy I live ;
Alas, sweet brooks ! do in my tears augment.
   Rocks, woods, hills, caves, dales, meads, brooks
      answer me :
Infected minds infect each thing they see.

              Finis.   *Sir Phil. Sidney.*

OF DISDAINFUL DAPHNE.

SHALL I say that I love you,
   Daphne disdainful ?
Sore it costs as I prove you,
   Loving is painful.

Shall I say what doth grieve me ?
   Lovers lament it.
Daphne will not relieve me ;
   Late I repent it.

Shall I die, shall I perish,
   Through her unkindness ?
Love, untaught love to cherish,
   Showeth his blindness.

Shall the hills, shall the valleys,
   The fields, the city,
With the sound of my outcries,
   Move her to pity ?

The deep falls of fair rivers,
　　And the winds turning,
Are the true music-givers
　　Unto my mourning ;

Where my flocks daily feeding,
　　Pining for sorrow
At their master's heart-bleeding,
　　Shot with Love's arrow.

From her eyes to my heartstring
　　Was the shaft lancèd ;
It made all the woods to ring,
　　By which it glancèd.

When this nymph had used me so,
　　Then she did hide her ;
Hapless I did Daphne know,
　　Hapless I spied her.

Thus turtle-like I wail'd me,
　　For my love's losing ;
Daphne's trust thus did fail me :
　　Woe worth such choosing !

　　　　Finis.　　*M. N. Howell.*

THE PASSIONATE SHEPHERD TO HIS LOVE.

COME live with me and be my love,
　And we will all the pleasures prove,
That valleys, groves, hills, and fields,
Woods, or steepy mountains yields.

And we will sit upon the rocks,
Seeing the shepherds feed their flocks,
By shallow rivers, to whose falls
Melodious birds sings madrigals.

And I will make thee beds of roses,
And a thousand fragrant posies,
A cap of flowers and a kirtle
Embroider'd all with leaves of myrtle;

A gown made of the finest wool,
Which from our pretty lambs we pull;
Fair lined slippers for the cold,
With buckles of the purest gold;

A belt of straw and ivy buds,
With coral clasps and amber studs;
And if these pleasures may thee move,
Come live with me and be my love.[1]

The shepherd swains shall dance and sing
For thy delights each May morning;
If these delights thy mind may move,
Then live with me and be my love.

Finis.   *Chr. Marlow.*

[1] After this stanza there follows in the second edition of
Walton's *Compleat Angler*, 1655 :—
        " Thy silver dishes for thy meat,
        As precious as the gods do eat,
        Shall on an ivory table be
        Prepared each day for thee and me." ·
(The poem was first published without the fourth and sixth
stanzas, and without the author's name, in *The Passionate
Pilgrim*, 1599. Textual variations are recorded in my edition
of Marlowe, vol. iii., pp. 283-4.)

THE NYMPH'S REPLY TO THE SHEPHERD.

IF all the world and love were young,
And truth in every shepherd's tongue,
These pretty pleasures might me move,
To live with thee and be thy love.

Time drives the flocks from field to fold,
When rivers rage, and rocks grow cold;
And Philomel becometh dumb;
The rest complains of cares to come.

The flowers do fade, and wanton fields
To wayward Winter reckoning yields;
A honey tongue, a heart of gall,
Is fancy's spring, but sorrow's fall.

Thy gowns, thy shoes, thy beds of roses,
Thy cap, thy kirtle, and thy posies,
Soon break, soon wither, soon forgotten,
In folly ripe, in reason rotten.

Thy belt of straw and ivy buds,
Thy coral clasps and amber studs,
All these in me no means can move,
To come to thee and be thy love.

But could youth last, and love still breed,
Had joys no date, nor age no need,
Then these delights my mind might move,
To live with thee and by thy love.

Finis.   *Ignoto.*

ANOTHER OF THE SAME NATURE MADE

SINCE.

COME live with me and be my dear,
  And we will revel all the year,
In plains and groves, on hills and dales,
Where fragrant air breeds sweetest gales.

There shall you have the beauteous pine,
The cedar, and the spreading vine ;
And all the woods to be a screen,
Lest Phœbus kiss my summer's queen.

The seat for your disport shall be
Over some river in a tree,
Where silver sands and pebbles sing
Eternal ditties with the spring.

There shall you see the nymphs at play,
And how the satyrs spend the day ;
The fishes gliding on the sands,
Offering their bellies to your hands.

The birds, with heavenly tunèd throats,
Possess woods' echoes with sweet notes,
Which to your senses will impart
A music to inflame the heart.

Upon the bare and leafless oak,
The ringdoves' wooings will provoke
A colder blood than you possess,
To play with me and do no less.

In bowers of laurel trimly dight,
We will outwear the silent night,
While Flora busy is to spread
Her richest treasure on our bed.

Ten thousand glowworms shall attend,
And all their sparkling lights shall spend,
All to adorn and beautify
Your lodging with most majesty.

Then in mine arms will I enclose,
Lily's fair mixture with the rose,
Whose nice perfections in love's play
Shall tune me to the highest key.

Thus as we pass the welcome night
In sportful pleasures and delight,
The nimble fairies on the grounds
Shall dance and sing melodious sounds.

If these may serve for to entice
Your presence to Love's paradise,
Then come with me and be my dear,
And we will straight begin the year.

Finis.   *Ignoto.*

TWO[1] PASTORALS UPON THREE FRIENDS MEETING.

JOIN, mates, in mirth to me,
  Grant pleasure to our meeting ;
Let Pan our good god see
How grateful is our greeting ;
  Join hearts and hands, so let it be,
  Make but one mind in bodies three.

Ye hymns and singing skill
Of god Apollo's giving,
Be press'd our reeds to fill
With sound of music living.
  Join hearts and hands, &c. ·

Sweet Orpheus' harp, whose sound
The stedfast mountains movèd,
Let here thy skill abound
To join sweet friends belovèd.
  Join hearts and hands, &c.

My two and I be met,
A happy blessed trinity,
As three most jointly set,
In firmest band of unity.
  Join hearts and hands, &c.

Welcome my two to me,   E. D. F. G. P. S.
The number best belovèd,
Within my heart you be
In friendship unremovèd.
  Join hands, &c.

     [1] This poem was added in ed. 1614.

Give leave your flocks to range,
Let us the while be playing
Within the elmy grange;
Your flocks will not be straying.
  Join hands, &c.

Cause all the mirth you can
Since I am now come hither,
Who never joy but when
I am with you together.
  Join hands, &c.

Like lovers do their love,
So joy I in your seeing;
Let nothing me remove
From always with you being.
  Join hands, &c.

And as the turtle-dove
To mate with whom he liveth,
Such comfort fervent love
Of you to my heart giveth.
  Join hands, &c.

Now joinèd be our hands,
Let them be ne'er asunder,
But link'd in binding bands
By metamorphosed wonder,
  So should our sever'd bodies three
  As one for ever joinèd be.
       Finis.   *Sir Phil. Sidney.*

THE WOODMAN'S WALK.

THROUGH a fair forest as I went
   Upon a summer's day,
I met a woodman quaint and gent,
   Yet in a[1] strange array.
I marvell'd much at his disguise,
   Whom I did know so well;
But thus in terms both grave and wise,
   His mind he 'gan to tell.
Friend, muse not at this fond array.
   But list awhile to me;
For it hath holp me to survey
   What I shall show to thee.
Long lived I in this forest fair,
   Till, weary of my weal,
Abroad in walks I would repair,
   As now I will reveal.
My first day's walk was to the court,
   Where beauty fed mine eyes;
Yet found I that the courtly sport
   Did mask in sly disguise.
For falsehood sat in fairest looks,
   And friend to friend was coy;
Court favour fill'd but empty books,
   And there I found no joy.
Desert went naked in the cold,
   When crouching craft was fed;
Sweet words were cheaply bought and sold,
   But none that stood in stead.

      [1] Ed. 1600 omits "a."

Wit was employ'd for each man's own,
  Plain meaning came too short;
All these devices seen and known,
  Made me forsake the court.
Unto the city next I went,
  In hope of better hap;
Where liberally I launch'd and spent,
  As set on fortune's lap.
The little stock I had in store.
  Methought would ne'er be done;
Friends flock'd about me more and more,
  As quickly lost as won.
For when I spent then they were kind,
  But when my purse did fail,
The foremost man came last behind;
  Thus love with wealth doth quail..
Once more for footing yet I strove,
  Although the world did frown,
But they before that held me up,
  Together trod me down.
And lest once more I should arise,
  They sought my quite decay;
Then got I into this disguise,
  And thence I stole away.
And in my mind, methought, I said,
  Lord bless me from the city!
Where simpleness is thus betray'd,
  And no remorse or pity.
Yet would I not give over so,
  But once more try my fate,
And to the country then I go,
  To live in quiet state.
There did appear no subtle shows,

But yea and nay went smoothly ;
But, Lord, how country folks can glose,
   When they speak most soothly[1] !
More craft was in a button'd cap,
   And in an[2] old wives' rail,
Than in my life it was my hap
   To see on down or dale.
There was no open forgery,
   But underhanded gleaning ;
Which they call country policy,
   But hath a worser meaning.
Some good bold face bears out the wrong,
   Because he gains thereby ;
The poor man's back is crack'd ere long,
   Yet there he lets him lie ;
And no degree among them all
   But had such close intending :
That I upon my knees did fall,
   And pray'd for their amending.
Back to the woods I got again,
   In mind perplexèd sore,
Where I found ease of all this pain,
   And mean to stray no more.
There city, court, nor country too,
   Can any way annoy me ;
But as a woodman ought to do,
   I freely may employ me.
There live I quietly alone,
   And none to trip my talk :
Wherefore when I am dead and gone,
   Think on the woodman's walk.
            . *Finis.*   *Shep. Tony.*

[1] Ed. 1614 "vntruely."   [2] Omitted in ed. 1614.

THYRSIS[1] THE SHEPHERD TO
HIS PIPE.

L IKE desert woods, with darksome shades
       obscurèd,
Where dreadful beasts, where hateful horror reigneth,
Such is my wounded heart, whom sorrow paineth.

The trees are fatal shafts, to death inurèd,
That cruel love within my breast maintaineth,
To whet my grief, when as my sorrow waneth.

The ghastly beasts my thoughts in cares assurèd,[2]
Which wage me war, while heart no succour gaineth,
With false suspect and fear that still remaineth.

The horrors, burning sighs by cares procurèd,
Which forth I send, whilst weeping eye complaineth,
To cool the heat the helpless heart containeth.

But shafts, but cares, but sighs, horrors unrecurèd,
Were nought esteem'd if, for these pains awarded,
My faithful love by her might be regarded.
              Finis.   *Ignoto.*

[1] This is a second copy, with slight variations, of *The Shepherd's Dump*, printed on p. 128.
[2] Ed. 1614 " assures."

AN¹ HEROICAL POEM.

MY wanton Muse that whilom wont to sing
   Fair beauty's praise and Venus' sweet delight,
Of late had changed the tenor of her string
To higher tunes than serve for Cupid's fight :
   Shrill trumpets' sound, sharp swords, and lances
     strong,
   War, blood, and death, were matter of her song.

The god of love by chance had heard thereof,
That I was proved a rebel to his crown ;
" Fit words for war," quoth he, with angry scoff,
" A likely man to write of Mars his frown ;
   Well are they sped whose praises he shall write,
   Whose wanton pen can nought but love indite."

This said, he whisk'd his party-colour'd wings,
And down to earth he comes more swift than thought ;
Then to my heart in angry haste he flings,
To see what change these news of wars had wrought.
   He pries, and looks, he ransacks ev'ry vein,
   Yet finds he nought, save love and lover's pain.

Then I that now perceived his needless fear,
With heavy smile began to plead my cause :
"In vain," quoth I, "this endless grief I bear,
In vain I strive to keep thy grievous laws,
   If after proof so often trusty found,
   Unjust suspect condemn me as unsound.

    ¹ This poem was added in ed. 1614.

" Is this the guerdon of my faithful heart ?
Is this the hope on which my life is stay'd ?
Is this the ease of never-ceasing smart ?
Is this the price that for my pains is paid ?
 Yet better serve fierce Mars in bloody field,
 Where death or conquest, end or joy doth yield.

" Long have I served ; what is my pay but pain ?
Oft have I sued ; what gain I but delay ?
My faithful love is quited with disdain,
My grief a game, my pen is made a play ;
 Yea, love that doth in other favour find,
 In me is counted madness out of kind.

" And last of all, but grievous most of all,
Thyself, sweet Love, hath kill'd me with suspect.
Could Love believe, that I from Love would fall ?
Is war of force to make me Love neglect ?
 No, Cupid knows my mind is faster set,
 Than that by war I should my love forget.

" My Muse indeed to war inclines her mind,
The famous acts of worthy Brute to write ;
To whom the gods this island's rule assign'd,
Which long he sought by seas through Neptune's spite :
 With such conceits my busy head doth swell,
 But in my heart nought else but love doth dwell.

" And in this war thy part is not the least ;
Here shall my Muse Brute's noble love declare ;
Here shalt thou see thy double love increased,
Of fairest twins that ever lady bare.
 Let Mars triumph in armour shining bright,
 His conquer'd arms shall be thy triumph's light.

R

"As he the world, so thou shalt him subdue,
And I thy glory through the world will ring,
So by my pains thou wilt vouchsafe to rue
And kill despair." With that he whisk'd his wing,
　And bid me write, and promised wishèd rest;
　But sore I fear false hope will be the best.
Finis.　　　　*Ignoto.*

AN EXCELLENT SONNET OF A NYMPH.

VIRTUE, beauty, and speech, did strike, wound,
　　charm,
My heart, eyes, ears, with wonder, love, delight;
First, second, last, did bind, enforce, and arm,
His works, shows, suits, with wit, grace, and vows'
　　might.

Thus honour, liking, trust, much, far, and deep,
Held, pierced, possess'd, my judgment, sense, and will,
Till wrongs, contempt, deceit, did grow, steal, creep,
Bands, favour, faith, to break, defile, and kill.

Then grief, unkindness, proof, took, kindled, taught,
Well grounded, noble, due, spite, rage, disdain;
But ah, alas! in vain, my mind, sight, thought,
Doth him, his face, his words, leave, shun, refrain.
　For nothing, time, nor place, can loose, quench, ease,
　Mine own, embracèd, sought, knot, fire, disease.
Finis.　　*Sir Phil. Sidney.*

A REPORT SONG IN A DREAM, BETWEEN
A SHEPHERD AND HIS NYMPH.

SHALL we go dance the hay?   The hay?
   Never pipe could ever play
     Better shepherd's roundelay.

Shall we go sing the song?   The song?
Never Love did ever wrong.
     Fair maids, hold hands all along.

Shall we go learn to woo?   To woo?
Never thought came ever too (?),
     Better deed could better do.

Shall we go learn to kiss?   To kiss?
Never heart could ever miss
     Comfort where true meaning is.

Thus at base they run,   They run,
When the sport was scarce begun ;
     But I waked,[1] and all was done.
        Finis.   *N. Breton.*

ANOTHER OF THE SAME.

SAY that I should say I love ye,
   Would you say 'tis but a saying?
But if Love in prayers move ye,
   Will you not be moved with praying?

[1] Ed. 1614 "awak't."

Think I think that Love should know ye,
　Will you think 'tis but a thinking?
But if Love the thought do show ye,
　Will ye loose your eyes with winking?

Write that I do write you blessèd,
　Will you write 'tis but a writing?
But if Truth and Love confess it,
　Will ye doubt the true inditing?

No, I say, and think, and write it,
　Write, and think, and say your pleasure;
Love, and Truth, and I indite it,
　You are blessèd out of measure.
　　　　　Finis.　　　　*N. Breton.*

THE[1] LOVER'S ABSENCE KILLS ME,
HER PRESENCE CURES[2] ME.

THE frozen snake, oppress'd with heapèd snow,
　By struggling hard gets out her tender head,
And spies far off, from where she lies below,
The winter sun that from the north is fled;
　But all in vain she looks upon the light,
　Where heat is wanting to restore her might.

What doth it help a wretch in prison pent,
Long time with biting hunger overpress'd,
To see without, or smell within, the scent
Of dainty fare for others' tables dress'd?
　Yet snake and pris'ner both behold the thing,
　The which, but not with sight, might comfort bring.

[1] This poem was added in ed. 1614.
[2] Old ed. "kils."

Such is my state, or worse, if worse may be ;
My heart oppress'd with heavy frost of care,
Debarr'd of that which is most dear to me,
Kill'd up with cold, and pined with evil fare ;
 And yet I see the thing might yield relief,
 And yet the sight doth breed my greater grief.

So Thisbe saw her lover through the wall,
And saw thereby she wanted that she saw ;
And so I see, and seeing want withal,
And, wanting so, unto my death I draw.
 And so my death were twenty times my friend,
 If with this verse my hated life might end.
     Finis.   *Ignoto.*

THE SHEPHERD'S CONCEIT OF
PROMETHEUS.

PROMETHEUS, when first from heaven high
 He brought down fire, ere then on earth unseen,
Fond of delight,[1] a satyr, standing by,
Gave it a kiss, as it like sweet had been.

Feeling forthwith the other burning power,
Wood with the smart, with shouts and shriekings shrill,
He sought his ease in river, field, and bower,
But for the time his grief went with him still.

---

[1] Hannah (in *Courtly Poets*) reads, from Harleian MS. 6910,
"fond of the light." It is certainly a plausible correction.

So silly I, with that unwonted sight,
In human shape an angel from above,
Feeding mine eyes, th' impression there did light,
That since I run and rest as pleaseth Love.
  The difference is, the satyr's lips, my heart;
  He for a while, I evermore have smart.
                    Finis.   *S. E. D.*

ANOTHER OF THE SAME.

A SATYR once did run away for dread,
   With sound of horn which he himself did blow;
Fearing and fear'd, thus from himself he fled,
   Deeming strange evil in that he did not know.

Such causeless fears when coward minds do take,
   It makes them fly that which they fain would have,
As this poor beast, who did his rest forsake,
   Thinking not why, but how himself to save.

Even thus might I, for doubts which I conceive
   Of mine own words, mine own good hap betray;
And thus might I, for fear of *may be*, leave
   The sweet pursuit of my desirèd prey.
     Better like I thy satyr, dearest DYER,
     Who burnt his lips to kiss fair shining fire.
                    Finis.   *Sir Phil. Sidney.*

THE SHEPHERD'S SUN.

FAIR nymphs, sit ye here by me,
  On this flowery green,
While we this merry day do see
  Some things but seldom seen.
Shepherds all, now come sit around
  On yon chequer'd plain,
While from the woods we hear resound
  Some comfort [1] for love's pain.
    Every bird sits on his bough,
    As brag as he that is the best.
    Then sweet Love reveal how
      Our minds may be at rest.
    Echo thus replied to me,
    Sit under yonder beechen tree,
    And there Love shall show thee
      How all may be redress'd.

Hark, hark, hark! the nightingale,
  In her mourning lay;
She tells her story's woful tale,
  To warn ye if she may:
"Fair maids, take ye heed of love,
  It is a perlous [2] thing;
As Philomel herself did prove,
  Abusèd by a king;
    If kings play false, believe no men,
    That make a seemly outward show;

---

[1] Ed. 1600, "come."
[2] So ed. 1600.—Ed. 1614, "perilous."

But caught once, beware then,
    For then begins your woe.
They will look babies in your eyes,
    And speak so fair as fair may be ;
But trust them in no wise.
      Example take by me."

" Fie, fie ! " said the threstle-cock,
    " You are much to blame,
For one man's fault all men to blot,
    Impairing their good name.
Admit you were used amiss
    By that ungentle king,
It follows not that you for this,
    Should all men's honours wring.
      There be good, and there be bad,
      And some are false, and some are true ;
      As good choice is still had
        Amongst us men as you.
      Women have faults as well as we,
      Some say for our one they have three.
      Then smite not, nor bite not,
        When you as faulty be."

" Peace, peace," quoth Madge-Howlet then,
    Sitting out of sight ;
" For women are as good as men,
    And both are good alike."
" Not so," said the little wren,
    " Difference there may be,
The cock alway commands the hen ;
    Then men shall go for me."

Then Robin Redbreast stepping in,
Would needs take up this tedious strife,
Protesting true loving
   In either lengthen'd life.
"If I love you, and you love me,
Can there be better harmony?
Then ending contending,
   Love must the umpire be."

Fair nymphs, Love must be your guide,
  Chaste, unspotted love ;
To such as do your thralls betide,
  Resolved without remove.
Likewise jolly shepherd swains,
  If you do respect,
The happy issue of your pains,
  True Love must you direct.
    You hear the birds contend for love,
    The bubbling springs do sing sweet love,
    The mountains and fountains
      Do echo nought but love.
    Take hands then, nymphs and shepherds all,
    And to this river's music's fall,
    Sing true love, and chaste love !
      Begins our festival.

           Finis.   *Shep. Tony.*

LOVE[1] THE ONLY PRICE OF LOVE.

THE fairest pearls that northern seas do breed,
　For precious stones from eastern coasts are sold ;
Nought yields the earth that from exchange is freed,
Gold values all, and all things value gold ;
　　Where goodness wants an equal change to make,
　　There greatness serves, or number place doth take.

No mortal thing can bear so high a price,
But that with mortal thing it may be bought ;
The corn of Sicil buys the western spice ;
French wine of us, of them our cloth is sought.
　　No pearls, no gold, no stones, no corn, no spice,
　　No cloth, no wine, of love can pay the price.

What thing is love, which nought can countervail ?
Nought save itself, ev'n such a thing is love.
All worldly wealth in worth as far doth fail,
As lowest earth doth yield to heaven above.
　　Divine is love, and scorneth worldly pelf,
　　And can be bought with nothing, but with self.

Such is the price my loving heart would pay ;
Such is the pay thy love doth claim as due.
Thy due is love, which I, poor I, essay,
In vain essay to quite with friendship true.
　　True is my love, and true shall ever be,
　　And truest love is far too base for thee.

1 This poem was added in ed. 1614.

Love but thyself, and love thyself alone,
For, save thyself, none can thy love requite;
All mine thou hast, but all as good as none,
My small desert must take a lower flight.
   Yet if thou wilt vouchsafe my heart such bliss,
   Accept it for thy prisoner as it is.

Finis.   *Ignoto.*

COLIN, THE ENAMOURED SHEPHERD,

SINGETH THIS PASSION OF LOVE.

O GENTLE Love, ungentle for thy deed,
    Thou makest my heart
    A bloody mark
With piercing shot to bleed.

Shoot soft, sweet Love, for fear thou shoot amiss,
    For fear too keen
    Thy arrows been,
And hit the heart where my belovèd is.

Too fair that fortune were, nor never I
    Shall be so blest,
    Among the rest,
That love shall seize on her by sympathy.

Then since with Love my prayers bear no boot,
    This doth remain
    To ease my pain,
I take the wound, and die at Venus' foot.

Finis.   *Geo. Peele.*

ŒNONE'S COMPLAINT, IN BLANK VERSE.

MELPOMENE, the Muse of tragic songs,
With mournful tunes, in stole of dismal hue,
Assist a silly nymph to wail her woe,
And leave thy lusty company behind.

Thou[1] luckless wreath ! becomes not me to wear
The poplar tree for triumph of my love,
Then as my joy, my pride of love is left,
Be thou unclothèd of thy lovely green.

And in thy leaves my fortunes written be,
And them[2] some gentle wind let blow abroad,
That all the world may see how false of love
False Paris hath to his Œnone been.

Finis.   *Geo. Peele.*

THE SHEPHERD'S CONSORT.[3]

HARK, jolly shepherds,
Hark yon lusty ringing !
How cheerfully the bells dance,
The whilst the lads are springing !

[1] So in *The Arraignment of Paris.—England's Helicon,*
"This."
[2] So in *The Arraignment.—E. H.,* "Then."
[3] This is the last poem in ed. 1600 of *England's Helicon.*
The poems that follow were added in ed. 1614.

Go we then, why sit we here delaying?
And all yond merry wanton lasses playing?
  How gaily Flora leads it,
    And sweetly treads it?
  The woods and groves they ring,
    Lovely resounding
  With echoes sweet rebounding.

           Finis.   *Out of M. Morley's*
                        Madrigals.

THYRSIS' PRAISE OF HIS MISTRESS.

ON a hill that graced the plain,
  Thyrsis sat, a comely swain,
  Comelier swain ne'er graced a hill;
Whilst his flock that wander'd nigh,
Cropp'd the green grass busily,
  Thus he tuned his oaten quill.

Ver hath made the pleasant field
Many several odours yield,
  Odours aromatical;
From fair Astra's cherry lip
Sweeter smells for ever skip,
  They in pleasing passen all.

Leafy groves now mainly ring
With each sweet bird's sonnetting,
  Notes that make the echoes long;
But when Astra tunes her voice,
All the mirthful birds rejoice,
  And are listening to her song.

Fairly spreads the damask rose,
Whose rare mixture doth disclose.
  Beauties pencils cannot feign ;
Yet if Astra pass the bush,
Roses have been seen to blush,
  She doth all their beauties stain.

Phœbus shining bright in sky
Gilds the floods, heats mountains high,
  With his beams' all-quick'ning fire ;
Astra's eyes, most sparkling ones,
Strikes a heat in hearts of stones,
  And inflames them with desire.

Fields are blest with flow'ry wreath,
Air is blest when she doth breathe ;
  Birds make happy ev'ry grove,
She each bird when she doth sing ;
Phœbus heat to earth doth bring,
  She makes marble fall in love.
Those, blessings of the earth, we swains do call ;
Astra can bless those blessings, earth and all.
              Finis.   *W. Browne.*

A DEFIANCE TO DISDAINFUL LOVE.

NOW have I learn'd with much ado at last
    By true disdain to kill desire ;
This was the mark at which I shot so fast,
  Unto this height I did aspire.
Proud Love, now do thy worst and spare not,
For thee and all thy shafts I care not.

What hast thou left wherewith to move my mind?
  What life to quicken dead desire?
I count thy words and oaths as light as wind,
  I feel no heat in all thy fire.
Go change thy bow, and get a stronger;
Go break thy shafts, and buy thee longer.

In vain thou bait'st thy hook with beauty's blaze,
  In vain thy wanton eyes allure;
These are but toys for them that love to gaze,
  I know what harm thy looks procure.
Some strange conceit must be devised,
Or thou and all thy skill despised.

                    Finis.   *Ignoto.*

AN EPITHALAMIUM, OR A NUPTIAL SONG,

APPLIED TO THE CEREMONIES

OF MARRIAGE.

Sunrising.   AURORA'S blush, the ensign of the day,
           Hath waked the god of light from Tithon's bower,
Who on our bride and bridegroom doth display
His golden beams, auspicious to this hour.
Strewing   Now busy maidens strew sweet flowers,
of flowers. Much like our bride in virgin state;
           Now fresh, then press'd, soon dying.
The death is sweet, and must be yours,
Time goes on crutches till that date,
  Birds fledged must needs be flying.

Lead on while Phœbus' lights and Hymen's fires
Inflame each heart with zeal to Love's desires.
.   Chorus.   *Io to Hymen! Pæans sing*
                To Hymen and my Muses' king!

Going to   Forth, honour'd groom ! behold, not far behind,
church.   Your willing bride led by two strengthless boys !
Bride-boys. For Venus' doves, or thread but single twined,
              May draw a virgin, light in marriage joys.
    Vesta grows pale, her flame expires,
    As ye come under Juno's fane
        To offer at Jove's shrine
    The sympathy of hearts' desires,
    Knitting the knot that doth contain
        Two souls in Gordian twine.
The rites are done ; and now, as 'tis the guise,
Love's fast by day a feast must solemnize.
            Chorus.   *Io to Hymen! Pæans sing*
                       To Hymen, and my Muses' king!

Dinner.   The board being spread, furnish'd with various plenties,
             The bride's fair object in the middle placed,
             While she drinks nectar, eats ambrosial dainties,
             And like a goddess is admired and graced.
    Bacchus and Ceres fill their veins,
    Each heart begins to ope a vent ;
    And now the healths go round ;
        Their bloods are warm'd, cheer'd are their brains,
        All do applaud their loves' consent ;
        So Love with cheer is crown'd.
Let sensual souls joy in full bowls, sweet dishes,
True hearts and tongues accord in joyful wishes.
            Chorus.   *Io to Hymen ! &c.*

Afternoon.	Now whiles slow hours do feed the time's delay,
Music.	Confused discourse, with music mix'd among,
	Fills up the semicircle of the day ;
	Now draws the date our lovers wish'd so long.
Supper.	A bounteous hand the board hath spread,
	Lyæus stirs their bloods anew ;
	All jovial, full of cheer.
Sunset.	But Phœbus, see, is gone to bed !
	Lo, Hesperus appears in view,
	And twinkles in his sphere !
	Now ne plus ultra ; end as you begin ;
	Ye waste good hours ; time lost in love is sin.

        Chorus. *Io to Hymen! &c.*

	Break off your compliment ; music, be dumb ;
	And pull your cases o'er your fiddles' ears ;
	Cry not "A[1] hall, a hall!" but chamber-room ;
	Dancing is lame ; youth's old at twenty years.
Going to	Matrons, ye know what follows next ;
bed.	Conduct the shamefaced bride to bed,
	Though to her little rest.
	Ye well can comment on the text,
	And, in love's learning deeply read,
	Advise and teach the best.
	Forward's the word ; y' are also in this arrant ;
	Wives give the word, their husbands give the warrant.

        Chorus. *Io to Hymen! &c.*

Modesty in	Now droops our bride, and in her virgin state
the Bride.	Seems like Electra 'mongst the Pleiades ;
	So shrinks a maid when her Herculean mate
	Must pluck the fruit in her Hesperides.

    [1] "A hall, a hall!" was the cry raised when a space was to
be cleared for the dancers.

        S

As she's a bride, she glorious shines,
　Like Cynthia, from the sun's bright sphere,
　　Attracting all men's eyes ;
But as she's virgin, wanes and pines,
　As to the man she approacheth near ;
　　So maiden glory dies.
But virgin beams no real brightness render,
If they do shine, in dark to show their splendour.
　　Chorus.　*Io to Hymen !　&c.*

Then let the dark foil of the genial bed
Extend her brightness to his inward sight ;
And by his sense he will be eas'ly led
To know her virtue by the absent light.

Bride-
points ;
garters.

　Youths, take his points, your wonted right ;
　And, maidens, take your due, her garters ;
　　Take hence the lights, begone !
Love calls to arms, duel his fight ;
Then all remove out of his quarters,
　　And leave them both alone ;
That with substantial heat they may embrace,
And know Love's essence, with his outward grace.
　　Chorus.　*Io to Hymen !　&c.*

Hence Jealousy, rival to Love's delight,
Sow not thy seed of strife in these two hearts ;
May never cold affect, or spleenful spite
Confound this music of agreeing parts ;
　But time, that steals the virtual heat
　Where nature keeps the vital fire,
　　(My heart speaks in my tongue,)

Supply with fuel life's chief seat
Through the strong fervour of desire :
   Love living, and live long !
And e'en as thunder riseth 'gainst the wind,
So may ye fight with age and conquer kind.
   Chorus. Io to Hymen ! Pæans sing
        To Hymen, and my Muses' king !
          Finis.   Christopher Brooke.

BARGINET, *bargeret, rustic song*, 46.
Braids, *deceits*, 147.

Chevisaunce, *wall-flower*, 31.
Circes, *old form of* Circe, 128.
Crare, *small boat*, 157.

Distain, *outdo, excel*, 67.

Fautrix, *patroness*, 93.
Force, *esteem, regard*, 56.
Forswat, *over-sweated*, 30.
Forswonk, *out-wearied*, 30.

Gar, *make, cause*, 37.

Hay, *a rustic dance*, 243.

I wus, *i-wis, assuredly*, 224.

Lawnd, *lawn*, 223.
Leese, *lose*, 55, &c.
Levin, *lightning*, 39.
Look babies in the eyes, *peer amorously into a mistress' eyes*,
     248.
Lure, *to train hawks to fly at lures (artificial birds)*, 56.

Medled, *mixed*, 29.

Orped, *stout, fierce*, 219.
Orpharion, *musical instrument resembling a lute*, 45.

Paunce, *pansy*, 31.
Peat, *pet*, 142.
Perdie, *verily (par Dieu)*, 176.
Perk, *perch*, 48.
Pheer, *mate*, 78.
Pile, *arrow-head*, 206.
Puttock, *kite*, 95.

Rail, *neck-cloth*, 238.
Refell, *refute*, 159.
Reny, *deny*, 75.

Sauncing-bell, *the little bell that called to prayers*, 106.
Sounded, *swooned*, 164.

Tho, *then*, 225.

Yfere, *together, in company*, 29.

CHISWICK PRESS :—C. WHITTINGHAM AND CO.,
TOOKS COURT, CHANCERY LANE.